The Lost Princess

Rita Akoto Coker

Afram Publications (Ghana) Limited

Published by:
Afram Publications (Ghana) Limited
P.O. Box M18
Accra, Ghana

Tel:	+233 302 412 561, +233 244 314 103
Kumasi:	+233 322 047 524/5
E-mail:	sales@aframpubghana.com
	publishing@aframpubghana.com
Website:	www.aframpubghana.com

Cover illustration and design by: Kwabena Opoku

First Published, 2014

ISBN: 9964 70 521 2

Dedication

For my three younger brothers Kofi Sarpong Akoto,
Andy Osei Akoto, and Akwasi Amankwaa Afrifah Akoto.
I wish you all very well.

Acknowledgement

To my great grandmother, the late Nana Amma
Adutwumwaa, Queen of Antoa, Kwabere, whose stories as a
princess while growing up inspired my books.

Prologue

January, 1698- Nton

It was a cold misty morning. The sun's rays were struggling to pierce through the thick opaque mist that covered the town of Nton. It was that kind of morning that often coaxed people to stick to their beds. The warriors of Nton, exhausted from chasing their enemies, (the Dromis and the Akyes), from the other side of the Pra River the previous day, stuck to their beds. Not the women however.

Adwoa Dapaa, the beautiful young wife of Elder Ntim, one of the advisors of Nana Karikari, Chief of Nton, was leading a procession of three other women to her farm this morning.

They shivered in their thin cloths but stubbornly trudged on carrying baskets and other farm implements on their heads. The young women in the village helped one another on their farms or traded in salt, materials and other goods from the coast. They chatted as they walked along.

"Ei, if it was not for the timely warning that the Atagyahene, Nana Osei Appiah, sent to our chief to return from the war with his warriors to defend our town, we would all be dead by now in our beds," said Akosua Amponsah.

"Akosua, those are my thoughts exactly," replied Adwoa Dapaa, shaking her head. "Imagine the fact that almost all our warriors were out of town; how would we have defended ourselves and our families?"

Afua Kobi the youngest and fourth woman burst out laughing, surprising her companions who stopped in their tracks to look at her.

"What is so funny Afua? Are you out of your mind laughing at this time?" admonished Maame Panin, the eldest among them.

Her rebuke sobered Afua immediately who apologised and explained herself, "Oh, don't get me wrong. I am not laughing because of the grave danger we would have been in but I just remembered what happened yesterday when the Akyes were fleeing before our warriors." She turned to scan the faces of her companions one by one to see if they understood her explanation. She met blank faces and hurriedly tried to remind them of the incident. "Have you all forgotten the screeching noises they were making like chickens in flight?" Comprehension dawned on the others who burst out laughing as they continued their slow progress towards the farm.

"Well, we had no way of reading your thoughts Afua so can you blame us for our initial reactions to your laughter?" asked Adwoa Dapaa.

Suddenly, she stopped when she saw the destruction of the crops on the farm. Afua Kobi walking directly behind her on the narrow path bumped into her and exclaimed, "Adwoa, what is wrong?" Speechlessly, Adwoa only pointed in the direction of the mangled crops.

"Hei, what happened here?" Afua wailed.

Maame Panin gently pushed her aside and moved to the front. She also stopped suddenly and with hands on her hips, started to nod as a thought occurred to her.

"What is it Maame?" asked Adwoa Dapaa.

"I think the fleeing warriors must have passed directly through here," she replied.

"You may be right, Maame. How else can you explain this mayhem done to the crops? All our hard labour has come to nothing." Akosua Amponsa opined angrily as her eyes swept over the uprooted yams and cassava on the farm that stretched miles from where they were standing. Their surprise and shock turned to anger as each one expressed her feelings over the devastation.

"Well, there's no point weeping over spilt milk. Let us move over the land to see what we can glean," Maame Panin urged as she took the lead. They all moved cautiously from one mound to the other picking up discarded yams and cassava. Adwoa's steps led her to her favourite spot, a cave by a palm nut tree. As she approached the cave, she thought she heard a faint sound. She stopped in her tracks wondering what the sound could mean but as she stopped, the sound stopped as well so she thought she was hearing things and dismissing the sound, continued towards the cave. As she got closer, she heard the sound again and felt frightened. Was that a goat bleating? How could a goat venture so far away from the nearest house in the town? As she was pondering over this, the sound came out louder, prompting her to call to her companions urgently.

"Afua! Akosua! Come over here!" When the others got to her side, she cautioned them into silence with her finger on her lips and whispered, "Listen." There was the sound again making Afua Kobi jump, almost knocking Adwoa to the ground.

"What do you think it is, Adwoa?" Akosua asked. By this time Maame Panin had joined them and Adwoa tried to explain what she had heard. Suddenly, a stronger yell made all of them alert. It was Maame Panin who first reacted, "I think it's coming from that cave. Let us go and find out."

Adwoa took the lead as they cautiously approached the cave. Then they heard whimpers and Maame Panin asked thoughtfully, "Could it be a baby?"

"A baby?" chorused the others.

"What will a baby be doing here, ...so far away from the town?" Adwoa asked anxiously.

Maame Panin nudged her to continue her walk. It was dark inside the cave but their eyes soon adjusted to the darkness as they followed the wails of what could either be a baby, a lamb, or a kid, depending on whatever each one was thinking. Then Adwoa saw it; a baby wrapped in a soft blanket and wailing its head off. They all stood gaping down at it. Then Adwoa slowly knelt down and touched the cheeks of the baby who immediately responded by turning its eyes and mouth towards the touch. When its eyes clashed with Adwoa's, the latter immediately fell in love with the baby. With misted eyes, she slowly stretched her hands and gathered the baby to herself; it immediately ceased crying. Her companions stood in wonder, robbed of speech as they watched Adwoa gently rock the baby. Maame Panin was the first to come out of the stupor saying, "A baby? Who could have brought this baby here?" The others shook their heads, as puzzled as Maame.

"It's too far away from the nearest house in the town, so how did it get here?" Akosua asked.

"Hm, could the …the fleeing warriors have brought it here?" asked Afua Kobi.

Akosua snorted in disgust and replied, "How can that be? Men don't go to war carrying babies?"

"Oh yes, their wives do," replied Maame Panin. "Don't you know that some of the commanders take their wives to war with them? So probably one of those women took her baby along." She ended her conjecture as they all quietly chewed on this piece of information.

"Still, why would she leave her baby behind then? It doesn't make sense, leaving a precious baby in what everyone knows is enemy territory."

An idea struck Maame suddenly as she clicked her fingers. "Or they could have stolen it!" She exclaimed looking directly from one woman to the other. She continued "Look at the blanket it is wrapped in; this is not an ordinary blanket." She touched it, it felt smooth and soft.

"This kind of blanket is skillfully woven and looks expensive. It is woven with silk thread which is different from the cotton one our local blanket weavers use. It could only have come from a wealthy owner."

Maame's statement attracted Adwoa's attention, who, by this time was engrossed in gently rocking the baby in her arms. She quietly responded, "Stolen? Probably. Or it.. could be a gift to me from God," she ended with a far-away look in her eyes.

Two pairs of eyes turned to her as her statement sank into their consciousness. They all stared at her in awe partly believing this because their friend had been unlucky in childbirth in her four-year marriage to her husband. She was young and beautiful and everyone had been wondering why she could not bear children. She had entered the marriage with high hopes and even though her husband doted on her and had not taken another wife, her constant regret had been her inability to give her husband a child. Her friends who were standing with her knew her monthly agony, every time she saw her monthly flow. As much as they sympathised with her, none could help her. So for them to hear such a statement from her really moved them and they sincerely hoped that Adwoa Dapaa had indeed received a gift from God.

Maame Panin moved to lay a comforting hand on Adwoa's hand saying, "Adwoa, that may be so, but we must first report this matter to our chief, Nana Karikari and see what will happen, hmm? Because '*Onyame nkrabea nni kwatibea*'. If this baby is really a gift to you from God, no one can take it away from you."

The others nodded in agreement and Akosua responded "Yes, I think that is what we must do, Adwoa. There is no harm in making sure that this baby has been abandoned before you can claim it as your own, alright?"

Adwoa Dapaa nodded as tears rolled down her cheeks. They all turned around and walked out of the cave after they had checked that nothing else was left behind by whoever had brought the baby there. Akosua and Afua quickly picked up their abandoned baskets, now filled with some yams and cassava and led the way into town.

Meanwhile, in the palace, Nana Karikari and his elders, as well as the captains of the warriors were gathered in the council room where they were discussing the war of the previous day.

"When will this war end, Nana?" asked Opanin Asase.

"Your guess is as good as mine. As long as the

Dromohene continues to oppress us, this war will continue. How can he make such demands on us? How can he ask us to continue to send our beautiful girls along with that huge brass pan full of gold dust? No, no this is too much." The chief's frustration was evident in his impatient pacing up and down.

"Nana, you've said it," replied Akuamoa Fofie, the head captain of the advance guard warriors known as *twafo*. "We will not give up till we have removed Nana Frimpon Manso's yoke from our necks!" This statement was greeted with a general murmur of assent.

"They have no choice; they have to succumb to Nana Osei Appiah's reign," added Elder Ntim.

"After all, he is not a just ruler. I hear that all his vassals from Wassa, Twifo and Aowin are also fed up with his oppressive rule. We also hear from authoritative sources that they are happy about this war we are waging against him."

"Then why don't they rise up and join us instead of hiding behind our war, Nana?" Ofori, another young elder asked, wildly gesturing to make his point.

"I wish I knew, Ofori. You all know the adage that "*Meka nipa nti na aboa huruye nni adamfo*". He wants to garner power for himself alone and so everyone hates him. Anyway, I believe that when they are defeated, they will find out that Nana Osei Appiah is a better ruler than Frimpong Manso," Nana Karikari said.

This was so because it was widely known at this time that under the Atagya monarchy, justice always prevailed and that claims by his subjects were listened to without discrimination of rank or title. He had also developed a strong political system for effective rule and justice by creating other sub-chiefs under him and delegating power to each at different levels of authority. The highest ranked sub-chiefs called *Amanhene* are the next in command to him and the *Nsafohene*, the military commanders are selected from among these. These *Amanhene* are chiefs in their own right and were directly responsible to him. He depended on these for advice and they helped him to formulate policies.

The next in rank Adikro were divisional sub-chiefs who held their lands absolutely, holding their titles based on conquests rather than as gifts from Nana Osei Appiah. These had other sub sub-chiefs under them known as Aberempon, who were the chiefs of smaller villages and towns. Nana Karikari of Nton was among the latter.

"The reason I called you here is for us to discuss the cost of this war upon us. As the tortoise says, 'Ntɛm yɛ, na ogom yɛ'; yes, speed is good, but so is deliberation".

This war is costing us resources and men since we have to contribute our quota of the '*apeatuo*', war tax. We also have to supply Nana Osei Appiah with warriors. Most important of all, the men can neither attend to their farms regularly nor go about their businesses peacefully, and have left all the farming and trading to the women who are supposed to take care of the home. Even the Akwamu traders fear to venture into this area. This is not good for us and I think we should put some measures of defense here to secure our town and our daily livelihood. We may soon return to the war front since I don't believe this war is over yet. Do you have any thoughts on what I have just said?" Nana Karikari asked his advisors. The council deliberated on this for some time and Opanin Nkansah, the oldest of the counsellors concluded by saying, "Nana, as usual, you have hit the nail on the head by your decisions. And going by our elders' saying that "*Tikoro nko agyina*'; you have consulted us so that we will have an agreement by consensus. I speak for all of us, that we support all your decisions completely…" He could not finish his sentence because of a commotion they heard outside the council doors.

◆ ◆ ◆

"What is that noise?" Nana Karikari asked, commanding one of the guards to go and check it out. Adwoa Dapaa and her three friends, followed by a small crowd, had entered the palace arguing and discussing the discovery of the four-month old baby. The guard returned to inform the chief and his elders. Elder Ntim, upon hearing his wife's name quickly got up followed by the others and they filed out to the verandah and watched the crowd approach. The chief instructed the guard to stop the crowd and usher only Adwoa Dapaa and her friends into the council room. Elder Ntim walked to his wife who had tears on her cheeks, and gave her a questioning look but his wife continued to weep silently shaking her head and handing the baby over to him. The man accepted the baby gingerly with surprise; and looked down at the sleeping baby, who was oblivious to all the confusion it had caused.

The chief motioned Elder Ntim to come forward as the others looked on in wonder and puzzlement. The women were asked to take their seats and Maame Panin narrated what had happened at the farm. Some of the counsellors reacted in anger, others in despair. There were exclamations of surprise from every one of them but the chief kept quiet, as he chewed thoughtfully on all that he had heard. He beckoned Opanin Nkansah and his linguist, Nana Bannie, to him. After consultations with them, Nana Karikari made this pronouncement;"Indeed, this is a great wonder. How this baby, whom we have now ascertained is a girl, got to this town is a great puzzle. But first, since we don't know the parents of this beautiful baby girl, I decree that the baby be given to Adwoa Dapaa to take care of till we find out more about her. *Okyeame*, you will order the gong gong to be sounded immediately throughout this town asking if anyone has lost a baby, and if they have, for them to come and see me. Because the old adage says '*Adekese nyera*', nothing valuable can be misplaced for long. If the parents are not found in this town, I will send messages to the chiefs of the surrounding towns and villages informing them of our discovery. We will then wait for six months. If after six months, no one comes forward to claim the baby, I'll then decide what to do. Meanwhile, Adwoa," she stood up as the chief addressed her. "Take proper care of this baby. Our elders say that *wohwe obi ade so yie a, na wodie yeyie*. Take proper care of this precious find and you will have good success of your own. She has no name now but you and your husband may decide to give her one pending the time her ancestry will be determined."

"That is the command of our chief, elders." Nana

Bannie emphasised what the chief had said as was customary for an *okyeame* to do and went to take the baby from Elder Ntim's arms. He walked over to Adwoa Dapaa and handed her the baby. By this time, Adwoa Dapaa was kneeling down to thank the chief and his elders for the decision. As she got up and took the sleeping baby from the arms of *Okyeame* Bannie, the tears flowed freely. Her husband helped her up and embraced her and the baby. Many an eye misted knowing what this gesture meant to their young councillor and his wife.

Chapter One

"Ah Gyakari, you've won again. I can't believe this!" cried Prince Osei, his younger brother, appealing to the others seated around the two of them under the hut at the lower court of the palace of Nana Karikari. They were playing a game of *oware* with their friends and cousins.

"Come on Osei, is this anything new?" laughed his older brother, Prince Gyakari, the heir apparent to the throne of Nton; he expected to succeed his uncle Nana Karikari. Their mother, *Ohemaa* Gyamfuaa, is the queen of Nton and a sister to the chief. She has three sons and a daughter with Opanin Daase, one of the chief's elders and Gyakari is the eldest. At eighteen, he stood over six feet tall with rippling muscles that any teenager would envy. These being the war years of Asante kingdom, he and his two brothers have been trained in various warfare techniques and have a daily routine of warfare training.

Their day begins at four in the morning when they are put through a drill of physical endurance, followed by gruelling practice with different weapons like guns, javelins, spears, bows and arrows. After four hours of practice, they would plunge into the cool brisk waters of River Ande, which flows behind the palace walls, and which they access through a side gate behind the palace from the lower court. They then take their breakfast at the twelve-seat dining table in the family hall. The hall is a large L-shaped room with floor-to-ceiling windows in the form of slits cut into thick walls of baked and polished mud. Inside the L-angle of this room, there are rugs of thick goat skins in the centre of the floor flanked by various shapes and sizes of stools, chairs and benches. On the walls hang different weapons used by their ancestors.

After breaking their fast, they are tested and tried on horseback riding, something Prince Gyakari mastered at age ten. He and his black destrier, Warrior, have grown together and know one another so well that the Prince easily gives different instructions to his horse by simply giving slight pressures to its sides with his strong legs. It is only after their lunch break that they have time to themselves to indulge in any kind of pastime that takes their fancy. Playing *oware* was one of their favourite past times, which Prince

Gyakari says relaxes his body and his mind and enables him to practise strategies to defeat his opponents. Because this game had no hidden information or written rules on how to play and win, one had to be able to logically interpret every puzzle presented to him by an opponent and Gyakari was very good at this. Gyakari believed in doing everything well and none of his brothers or cousins could beat him at any game, including drafts.

On this day, after teasing his younger brother, he eased his strong body off the bench they had been sitting on, stretched his arms and flexed his powerful muscles. He stood taller than any of his brothers or cousins. Handsome and dark with an aquiline nose inherited from his mother, his dimples were so deep that they flashed on his handsome face even with the faintest hint of a smile. Deep, dreamy, penetrating eyes covered with long lashes that seemed to see through everything completed his perfect facial features. With a broad chest, narrow hips, a taut, flat stomach, well-toned thighs, and well-sculptured feet, he was the envy of his contemporaries and the cynosure of all female eyes, particularly one girl, Akua Bakoma.

She was a young and beautiful girl; she who had been found on a cold, misty morning in a cave on the farm of her parents. Yes, that baby girl whose biological parents were never found had grown into one of the most beautiful girls of her time. With a heart-shaped face and a cylindrical neck, she had long black silky hair, always plaited and hanging down her neck. Even at age sixteen, her beauty shone like a star. White pearly teeth shone out of light thinned lips every time she smiled. Her eyebrows fanned out like ferns over her large beautiful eyes. She always walked gracefully with a poise that was in-born which often drew comments from both adults and children alike that she carried herself like a princess.

Only few inhabitants of Nton at this time knew that she wasn't the biological daughter of Elder Ntim and Maame Adwoa Dapaa. She had been brought up practically at the palace where her mother Adwoa served as one of the queen's chambermaids. Being the same age as the queen's only daughter Princess Boatemaa, Akua Bakoma had grown up a pampered child loved by all who came across her due to her sweetness of temperament. She had particularly been close to Prince Gyakari, who, as they were growing up had always soothed her whenever she bruised her knee while playing with the young royals. As such, the prince had become very possessive of her and her attentions. Recognising her extraordinary beauty for the first time a year ago had shifted something inside of him; feelings other than brotherly ones had replaced his affections for her. Since that day, he could no longer feel free in her presence and had tried as much as possible to avoid her but to no avail since they were being thrown together constantly at the palace.

Another problem he could not avoid was that Bakoma was always coming to him, seeking him out with one problem or the other, something she had been doing since they were children. He had no way of knowing whether Bakoma found him attractive as other girls did but he was indeed under her spell, as were his cousins, Nana Karikari's sons. But as they all had seen the way Gyakari behaved towards her, they had silently suppressed any romantic feelings they might have had towards her and they covered their wistfulness by constantly teasing Prince Gyakari about her.

Chapter Two

On this day in 1714, Akua Bakoma carried a tray with tall glasses of cool coconut juice to the group at the lower court. With a black and white cloth tied securely across her ample bosom, she walked sedately towards them as all eyes turned towards her. Prince Gyakari had not seen her as he had been busy exercising his muscles; not hearing the normal words of admiration from his cousins, he had turned to find out why they were all silent. He followed the direction of their eyes to see Bakoma walking towards them with a bright smile, her eyes fixed on him. The others on seeing this, started teasing him again and to cover up some deep feelings which her presence always evoked in him, Prince Gyakari barked at her, "Why are you the one bringing us refreshment? Where are the servants?" He scowled at her. Her beautiful smile vanished and in confusion she looked at the others before her eyes settled on Prince Gyakari.

"My...my lord", using the title for the first time, "Your mother the queen asked me to bring your refreshment. I...I don't know why..." her voice faltered.

Prince Osei quickly stood up from where he was seated, took the tray from her, and set it down. He then draped his arm around her shoulders and walked her out of the lower court. Everyone was puzzled, including the guards. They had never seen their young lord speak to Bakoma this way before. Prince Prempeh, the youngest of the queen's children was the only one who dared to rebuke his older brother. "What is wrong with you, Gyakari? What did Bakoma do for you to disgrace her like that? This is not right. I'll tell mother about it!" He promptly left to go and do just that. Prince Gyakari was stunned at his own reactions. He wondered why he had reacted like that towards Bakoma. Then it dawned on him that he disliked the way his cousins Princes Bonsu, Kyeretwie and Opoku, and his own brother Prince Osei had been staring at her. Jealousy? The green-eyed monster had caught him unawares!

"Me jealous?" he mused. Then realisation dawned on him. "Oh God, I lo...love her..." He sat down in a daze finally giving a name to the strange feelings he had had for Bakoma for about a year.

Meanwhile, Prince Osei had managed to calm Bakoma down and she had returned to the room she shared with Princess Boatemaa at the palace. This room, like the others was luxuriously furnished; plush goat skins of different colours carpeted the floor, wall to wall. She went straight to lie down on one of the intricately carved canopied beds that dominated the room, still puzzled by Prince Gyakari's attitude towards her. She loved him as a brother and felt closer to him more than even his sister Princess Boatemaa whom she regarded as her closest friend. She tried to figure out what she had done to earn his censure. She didn't want to lose his friendship and yet didn't know what to do. She was in this mood when Princess Boatemaa entered with her maid. She ran to her with concern having heard Prince Prempeh's report to their mother.

"Bakoma, are you all right? I just heard."

"Heard what?" she asked turning her head to look at her friend.

"What Gyakari did to you. What happened?"

She shrugged and replied, "I don't know." She paused and then continued, "Perhaps I shouldn't have obeyed your mother, the queen…"

"Don't be silly. Why ever not? It's not your fault but Gyakari's. Ah, I feel like boxing his arrogant ears." This statement brought a chuckle from Bakoma erupting into laughter as the others joined her.

Bakoma could not imagine the diminutive Boatemaa stretching to box the ears of her brother who stood at least two heads taller than her. But Princess Boatemaa was satisfied that she had been able to make her closest friend laugh. Afrah, Princess Boatemaa's eighteen-year old maid looked at the two while dwelling on her own thoughts about Prince Gyakari who had abruptly ended his liaison with her a few months back. She had wondered whether the prince had found interest in another girl. Now hearing about the Gyakari-Bakoma drama, it occurred to her that Bakoma could be his new love interest. And she suspected his reported actions could be a mark of jealousy.

"But they're like brother and sister," she thought. "It can't be. Oh no, I don't stand a chance if she's the one he wants…"

Her thoughts were broken into by her mistress. "Afrah, Afrah, what's wrong with you? Have you heard a single word I've spoken to you?"

"Oh Nana, sorry. I didn't hear what you said."

"Are you day dreaming again? Is my brother giving you also a hard time?" she asked, with a teasing smile.

Bakoma turned to look at Afrah with a smile as

well.

Afrah replied, shuffling in embarrassment, "Nana no. We're no longer an item."

"Hmm, is that why you've been day-dreaming so much of late? What happened, tell me?" her mistress asked with curiosity.

Afrah shrugged, "I don't know. Nana please don't worry about me. It's Bakoma we should be concerned about now..." she quickly replied wanting to divert attention from herself.

"Oh well, if you say so" and turning to Bakoma said, "Bakoma, come. Let's go for a swim, I'm sure it will cool you down." Bakoma eased up but shook her head saying, "I'm not angry, I'm just puzzled, that's all. So don't worry about me, ok?"

"Are you sure?" Then turning to her maid, the princess said, "Afrah, I think only you and I know the hot temper this one over here has," pointing at Bakoma with a smile. "Looking at her, one can never tell."

"Oh Boatemaa, stop teasing," Bakoma pleaded with her. "I am all right, really. I would have told you the truth because you're more than a sister to me." The two hugged and left for the riverside.

Meanwhile, Prince Gyakari had answered his mother's summons. He had left for her quarters, followed by his *gyaase*, Agyei, the personal guard. His mother sent away the guard as well as all her maids and counsellors, one of them being Adwoa Dapaa, to prevent anyone hearing what she wanted to discuss with her son. She didn't want any false rumour flying around about his son.

With all her heart, Queen Gyamfuaa loved Akua Bakoma like her own and she had always had this intuition that she must have been stolen from another royal household, even though she had often dismissed this thought by admonishing herself that it was out of her own wishful desire for her son to marry Bakoma that might have made her feel that way. But she knew that nothing would make her feel better if it were possible for them to marry. She wondered whether it was this secret desire of hers that had prompted her to send Bakoma to her son that afternoon but she had not counted on the outcome, the results of which had alarmed her. The fact is, Gyakari as the heir, could only marry a princess as a first wife and if he chose, he could then have many concubines and wives later who would not necessarily be of royal birth.

Chapter Three

She asked her son to sit down when he entered her room. "No mother, I don't want to," Gyakari replied and began to pace the floor. His mother watched him for a while and asked, "What is the matter? Why won't you sit down?" Her son turned to her noting the anxiety in her questions. He looked at her for a moment and asked, "Mother, is it really true that my first wife has to be a princess?" The queen was taken aback by his direct question but she didn't show it, wondering what had prompted his question, so she answered cautiously. "Well…yes you know this son but you can have as many wives as you want after that, not counting the concubines of course," she smiled, trying to defuse the tension in the room.

Gyakari resumed pacing like a lion in a cage. Several thoughts were cruising through his mind; he knew that he didn't want Akua Bakoma as a second wife, let alone a concubine, but as his soul mate. He therefore decided to beard the lioness. He stopped suddenly and announced, "Mother I love Akua Bakoma." He was in turn surprised that his mother didn't look surprised. She did not say anything but kept looking steadily at him. That was her heart's desire as well but she also knew the consequences of not following tradition. She was rudely awakened to the problems that could face her son and Akua Bakoma if she encouraged any union between them. She therefore decided to nip everything in the bud, but in a very careful manner, knowing his temper.

Gyakari had seen the look in his mother's eyes suddenly solidify into steel and his heart pumped with speed. "Mother, did you hear what I said?" He asked as he approached her. He knelt before her taking her hands in his own. She only nodded.

"Then say something. What do you think? What am I to do?"

"Gyakari, first things first. So you love her, fine and so...?" she asked nonchalantly, then continued "So do you love other girls."

"No mother. This is different. This feeling I have for Bakoma is...is different from any other feelings I've ever had for any girl." He stood up slowly and began to pace once again, then turning said with a light chuckle said, "It's ironic that I showed it in the wrong way this afternoon."

"Oh that. Yes, that's why I sent for you in the first place. Tell me, what really happened down there, son?"

He didn't respond immediately but walked slowly to the window facing the courtyard and looking down, heaved a big sigh. "Mother, I don't really know. One moment I was in a daze about her beauty and in another moment I was screaming at her." He finished as he turned to the queen, "What do you think of that, mother, heh?"

"You tell me, son," the queen gently prodded knowing the agony her son must be going through.

He paused for a moment looking at her and replied slowly, "I think I was jealous, mother. Very jealous!" He ended remembering the intense feeling he had felt at the time.

"Jealous? Why?" The queen asked, puzzled. "Because everyone was staring at her with such ...such hunger and...and adoration in their eyes and I couldn't stand it. I got angry at her thinking that she was deliberately leading everyone on. You know Bonsu, Osei, Kyeretwie and even the guards! Can you imagine that? And I got upset. I couldn't help myself." By this time, he had returned to his mother and sat down.

"What was her reaction, Gyakari?" He turned away

from her probing eyes and with anguish whispered, "She was confused and started to cry." Turning to her, he asked, "What will I do now, mother? She must hate me now." The queen stood up and walked to him, and looking down said, "Oh I don't think so, son. Bakoma likes you. She adores you. You are her warrior, remember, hmm?" She smiled and Prince Gyakari remembered the many times he had gone to her defence when they were growing up.

"Well, I don't know. Probably I should send her a present to pacify her. What do you think, mother?"

"A present? Can't you just talk to her?", she asked knowing the implications of her son sending Bakoma a present. He stood up, looked down at her, and said, "No, I just can't talk to her because all of a sudden, I feel as if she's beyond my reach. I'll feel awkward apologising to her. A prince does not apologise, remember? So I think a present will be better." He ended, appealing for his mother's approval.

"All right. What kind of present are you thinking about?" Thinking as she walked back to her seat that she may be able to influence the outcome in order not to encourage any hopes of a relationship between the young ones. "The last time the Akwamu traders passed through here, I bought some yards of aquamarine silk material I wanted to surprise Boatemaa with but

I think I'll give it to Bakoma and buy another one for Boatemaa later. What do you think?" "Hmm, all right if you feel that way but remember, talking to her would be better. So think about it." "Thank you, mother. I'll do that when I have enough courage," he said, smiling for the first time since he entered the room.

"Courage? Gyakari, you a coward? That will be the day!" she laughed and Gyakari joined her. "Mother don't tease. I really don't know what's wrong with me. I would never have thought that I could be tongue-tied before a girl. Me, and especially with Bakoma? No, I never thought I'll see the day. Bakoma has been like a sister to me all this time and yet...hmm" He ended the statement in uncertainty, staring into space with arms akimbo and shaking his head.

The queen knew then that her son had fallen hard for Bakoma and wondered where it would end since she knew she would have to do everything in her power to discourage them. With a sigh, she got up, wishing him luck. She watched his retreating back with concern and thought about discussing the matter with her husband later that day.

Chapter Four

Akua Bakoma and Princess Boatemaa had returned from swimming later that day to supper. Everyone had been in high spirits at the dining table except Bakoma and Prince Gyakari. The queen had watched the two and had seen the fearful glances Bakoma had been throwing at her son and how her son had struggled to ignore her. Bakoma couldn't eat. She toyed with her food. She was hurting. She couldn't understand the reason why her childhood hero would suddenly turn against her. What puzzled her most was his pretence that she didn't exist by his refusal to look her way. A sharp pain went through her when this realisation dawned on her. "It can't be," she thought. "Everything else but that." She desperately needed his attention. She knew she could never stand his indifference. She almost choked on her food, causing the queen to ask , "Are you all right, Bakoma?" She nodded and quickly swallowed what was in her mouth and asked to be excused. Every eye turned to her, including Opanin Daase, the queen's husband and the father of her children. He asked his wife, "What's wrong with Bakoma, Gyamfuah?" She answered cautiously turning to look at Gyakari. "I'm not very sure but I think Gyakari has something to do with it."

Every eye now turned to the prince who, in the midst of taking food to his mouth paused when he heard his name mentioned. He cast a look of betrayal at his mother but heard his father asking, "Gyakari, what is the matter? Did you two quarrel?" Before he could answer, Prince Prempeh replied, "He shouted at her this afternoon. It was awful, Papa. He disgraced her in front of everyone, including the guards."

Prince Gyakari cast him a dark look which cleared immediately he heard his father's voice again. "You haven't answered my question? Did you two quarrel, Gyakari?"

"No Papa," he whispered.

"Then what happened?"

"I don't really know Papa. Look, I'll go and apologise to her." He said, standing up at the same time to forestall any further queries from his father. In a reproachful tone his father replied "You better go and do so quickly son because I have never seen Bakoma like this before."

When Bakoma returned to her room, she found a parcel on her bed. She was surprised upon opening it and gasped with pleasure. "Who could have sent this to me?" She asked herself, running her hands over the smooth, silky material. She forgot momentarily the reason why she had returned to her room, glorying in the perfection of the shining material and rubbing a piece of it against her cheeks. She was so caught up in this that she didn't hear Prince Gyakari enter the room.

He stood watching her for a moment, happy that she loved the present. Agyei, his bodyguard wanted to say something but he hushed him up and this sound attracted Bakoma's attention, and she quickly stood up from the bed. She was surprised to see Gyakari inside their room because he hardly came there. She was overcome with apprehension and didn't know what to think. She watched him in his black and white smock, standing tall and strong like an ebony tree. His dark piercing gaze sought hers and as their eyes clashed, Bakoma knew that she was lost.

"What? What is this?" she thought brushing her braids with a nervous hand. Trying to identify what was happening to her, she went on "What is this I'm feeling?" Yet she couldn't tear her eyes away from his gaze. The message in his eyes was quite different from what she had known over the years. She could see adoration and something else in his eyes. What could it be?

◆ ◆ ◆

They looked at each other for only seconds but to Bakoma, it was like eternity. An eternity involving only the two of them. Agyei felt the charged atmosphere and felt he had to leave the two alone. It was his request to withdraw that broke the magical under currents between the two. Prince Gyakari entered and closed the door. He slowly approached Bakoma whose beauty drew him like a moth to a flame. She in turn felt trapped and couldn't move. She was mesmerized by his beautiful eyes as he approached. He stood before her and took her right hand in his left and opened his mouth to speak but found himself drawing Bakoma into his arms instead. They clung to one another and he felt her shiver in his arms. No words were needed to explain how they felt about each other. They just held each other for sometime before Gyakari felt strong enough to set her away from him. Bakoma turned away from him and walked slowly to a stool by one of the windows; she sat down because her legs felt wobbly.

"God, what has come over me?" Her mind wondered in confusion.

Prince Gyakari watched the conflicting emotions dancing over her beautiful delicate features and slowly walked over to her.

"Bakoma, I'm really sorry about what happened this afternoon." He stopped when she

looked up at him. She knew he was sincere but she couldn't continue looking at him and ducked her head. Gyakari didn't like that.

"Bakoma, look at me." He commanded gently and waited like eternity till she did so before he continued, "I don't know what came over me. Please, forgive me," he ended in a whisper surprised at himself that he Gyakari was actually apologising to a girl and feeling better doing so. She nodded blinking as unshed tears fell on her cheeks. This brought Gyakari to his knees before her and gathering her hands in his own promised, "I'll never hurt you like that again. Please forgive me." She could still not say anything but continued to weep silently, bravely trying to smile but failing. This sent a crushing pain through Gyakari and he stood up quickly pulling her into his arms once more as his mouth crashed on hers. She resisted at first but later gave in to the onslaught of this fury mixed with something she couldn't name in this her first ever kiss. She yielded to him as he pressed her closer to him. Gyakari knew that instant that he could never let her go and that whatever it took, he was going to marry her as his soul mate. They broke the kiss as Bakoma came up for air looking strangely at Gyakari and looking for answers.

"I love you, Bakoma. Believe me, I do."

Chapter Five

Akua Bakoma continued to stare at Prince Gyakari as if she was seeing him for the first time. Her only response to his declaration was to reach out and touch his cheeks lightly but she quickly removed her hand as if she had been burnt and turned away.

"What is it Bakoma? I said I'm in love with you. Did you hear me?"

She nodded, wrapping her two arms around her as if she had taken a sudden chill. Her tears began to flow anew and this time, she sobbed aloud. Gyakari was alarmed and not knowing what to do, just pulled her arms away gathering her back into his arms and patting her back as if she were a child.

"Talk to me Bakoma. What is it?" He pleaded with her as he led her back to the window seat. Seated side by side with her hand in his, she looked up at him and asked, "Do you know the implications of what you've just said, Gyakari?"

He nodded and replied "Yes."

"Then you know that I can't love you back…because I can never marry you."

"Can never…" Gyakari started but she interrupted him saying "Oh I know you can marry me as a second wife not as the first. But I can never ever share you with another. No, never!" She ended with flashing eyes and got up so suddenly that Gyakari was shocked.

Bakoma knew that as a first wife, she had the power to decide who her husband should or should not marry as her second and she could always persuade him not to marry another wife. She knew that as a second wife, she would be powerless to do so and the thought of sharing him was unthinkable. Gyakari was shocked, seeing Bakoma's temper in action for the first time. He had never imagined that she would be so passionate about anything and wondered what he was getting himself into because the wife of the next chief of Nton has to be docile, as far as he was concerned. There can never be another hot tempered person in his life if he could help it. But was she docile? He sat for a moment looking at her back and then slowly stood up. He went to stand right behind her and pulled her against his strong body.

"Bakoma, I have no intention of having another wife

if you consent to be my wife," he stated emphatically. She quickly turned around to face him in exasperation.

"Gyakari, what's wrong with you? You are the heir and according to tradition, you can't break it and I won't be the cause of you breaking with our tradition." She ended decisively, turning and walking away from him again. Gyakari became frustrated. His head knew she was making sense but his heart was determined not to see it. Oh true, they could become lovers but where would it end? His hold over her would be tenuous at best since another man could claim her as his wife. He loved her too much to make her his concubine. He wanted the best life for her and yet, he knew he had to do something or lose her forever to another. He became desperate. He needed to do something that would bind her to him but he also knew that what he had in mind would forever turn her against him so he decided on another course of action.

"Bakoma, look at me," he commanded urgently this time. She turned and did so. As their eyes met, he asked, "Do you believe that I love you and I'll do anything for you?" She hesitated but knew instantly that he was sincere so she nodded and swallowed hard as she watched him remove one of his two copper necklaces around his neck. He approached her and moved to placed it around her neck. She was shocked because this symbolised a betrothal and it couldn't be…

"No, Gyakari. I can't accept this, no…" she pushed him away.

"Bakoma, look at me. Do you at least care a little for me?" She stared at him and knew that she more than cared for him. She loved him as well; this had become clearer since their encounter in that room but she knew it shouldn't be, it mustn't be and yet… She didn't say anything. She merely nodded.

"Then just wear this for me. I know what others will say but please I need to do this. I don't want to lose you. Ever."

"But what about your betrothal to…"

"Betrothal to whom?" He asked with one of his deadly scowls. She knew instantly that she had made a mistake. She had let the cat out of the bag prematurely realising that he was not aware of what had been happening about his own marriage. Bakoma had heard a few days back from her mother that plans were being made to look for a suitable princess for him to marry. He took hold of her shoulders asking again, "Betrothal to whom Bakoma?"

"Oh forgive me, my lord. I shouldn't have said that. Please forget I said anything." He stared at her and knew that she knew something but decided not to pursue the matter since he felt there was no time for that so he continued to press his suit.

"All right, if you won't wear my necklace, then entwine it around your wrist as a bracelet. How about that?" and proceeded to do just that. Bakoma looked at her left wrist and looked up at him. As he looked into her eyes he said, "As from this day onwards, you are mine, Bakoma. My seal is upon you and I won't tolerate anyone, I mean any man coming near you. Do you get my meaning?" A lump had formed in her throat. Oh, how she longed just to be his. She swallowed hard and nodded. He took her face in his large warm palms and whispered, "Trust me. I'll take care of everything. Don't be afraid, all right?"

Oh she knew she could trust Gyakari. She had done that all her life. He had always made things right for her as they were growing up. With Gyakari, she could never be afraid of anything. He was her knight in shining armour and had always been. So she nodded again and yielded once more to his gentle kiss which immediately turned into something else. He kissed her in desperation; his kiss demanded acquiescence and she just had to respond. All that she couldn't say was translated in her response to his kiss. She clung to him thinking that even if it were a dream, she would take her chances with him and when he was out of reach, day dream about this moment forever.

They were suddenly interrupted when they heard Princess Boatemaa's query to Agyei at the door to her chambers. Gyakari reluctantly released her and whispered to her again of the promise of his love for her and left passing a puzzled Princess Boatemaa at the door without a word to her.

Bakoma walked over to her bed in a daze not being able to comprehend what had just happened between her and Prince Gyakari. Could it be true? Maybe she was just dreaming but she looked down at her left wrist and saw his seal and realised that it wasn't a dream after all. She quickly hid her left hand.

"Oh God! Gyakari loves me. I can't believe it. I must have loved him all my life and wasn't even aware of it till tonight...". Her musings were interrupted when Princess Boatemaa entered with her maid.

"Bakoma, did Gyakari apologise to you?" she asked, sitting down beside her on her bed.

She turned with a smile towards her friend replying, "He did, but how did you know?"

"Well Papa ordered him to do so after you ran out of the dining room. What happened for you to run away like that?" Boatemaa asked with concern.

"I felt hot all of a sudden...and just...decided that I

needed some air and so left. That's all."

She had to lie because she knew that no one must know what was happening between her and Gyakari, not even her best friend.

"Hmm," was all the princess could say not convinced but knowing that Bakoma wasn't in the mood to talk so she decided to drop the subject. Then she saw the silk material.

"Bakoma! This is exquisite. Where did you get this material from?"

She shrugged replying "I don't know myself. When I got here, it was lying on my bed."

"I wonder who must have sent this or do you have a secret admirer I don't know of?" Boatemaa teased her. Bakoma started at this but realised that the princess was in her usual teasing mood and ignored the question. But the princess was anxious to find out so turning to her maid said, "Afrah, go and find out who sent this material to Bakoma." Afrah returned with the news that the guard downstairs said Prince Gyakari's guard brought it when they were at supper.

Bakoma was pleasantly surprised to hear this.

"Gyakari sent you this, Bakoma?" She asked with surprise and continued with "But why? Oh I know! It's his way of apologising for his rotten behaviour towards you this afternoon. So you see, don't worry.

Gyakari has always adored you, always showing you preference over all of us. That was why his behaviour towards you this afternoon puzzles me. Anyway, never mind. I'm sure you like it. Don't you Bakoma? If nothing can make you forgive him, this material surely can. Don't you think so Afrah?" she appealed to her maid for support after not receiving any response from Bakoma. Bakoma was clearly speechless and didn't know what to say but had to agree with the princess' assessment. Secretly, she was happy in the knowledge that Gyakari really cared for her.

Chapter Six

Nana Osei Appiah had come into an alliance with the Akwamus through the new Akwamuhene, Nana Addo. The Akwamus were well known traders supplying the Atagyas with firearms and munitions and this alliance had helped the Atagyas in the defeat of Dromo in November 1701 when the Akwamus effectively cut off the supply of guns and gun powder to the Dromos.

Yet with all this, the Atagya traders found it difficult to gain easy access to the coast therefore there were in constant battles with the Aowins and Twifos to secure this access from 1714 onwards.

The town of Nton being a tributary state of the Atagyahene, had to send their share of warriors to support these wars. Nana Karikari had effectively done this constantly and in preparation for another war, he had marshalled the warriors of Nton who were being drilled for the war and among them were

Princes Gyakari, Osei and their cousins Princes Bonsu and Kyeretwie. They were all busy training but Prince Gyakari under the tutorship of the captain of his division was distracted. The reason was very clear because since his encounter with Bakoma, he had not been able to see her alone. He had discovered that she was doing so deliberately. She was avoiding him and was always making sure that someone was with her at all times. What he couldn't understand was her reason for avoiding him.

◆ ◆ ◆

What he didn't know was that after his meeting with her that night when he had declared his love for her, she had not been able to sleep. So it had been a red-eyed, restless girl who had left the palace early the next morning to go and seek the counsel of her mother.

Maame Adwoa Dapaa and her husband lived in a modest house about one hundred and fifty metres from the palace. When she got home, her mother was already up and was washing her face when she noticed her daughter. She was surprised because since age ten, when the queen had asked Bakoma to move to live within the palace to keep her daughter Princess

Boatemaa company, her daughter had never sought her this early. Maame Adwoa wiped her face and stood watching as Bakoma approached her. She noticed her red eyes and the careless way she was dressed this morning. Her manner of dress really alarmed her because Bakoma always dressed impeccably and was very careful about her appearance at all times. The next surprise for her was the way Bakoma threw her arms around her and started sobbing. This was a stunner because even as a child, Bakoma hardly exhibited this kind of emotional attitude.

"Bakoma, Bakoma what is it? What has happened, child?" She asked anxiously.

"Oh mother, just hold me. I don't... don't know what I'm going to do now."

Her mother set her away from herself, staring at her wet face and trying to figure out what Bakoma was saying. All sorts of ideas started running through her mind. She knew Bakoma's beauty could endanger her especially where the four young princes, comprising of the queen's children and those of the chief at the palace were concerned, but she had always believed that they all regarded her fondly as a sister and yet... Then a thought occurred to her and in anxiety, she asked, "Did any of the princes...eh ...eh attack you?"

"No mother."

"Then what is it? Tell me. Come over here." She led her to a stool.

They both sat down. "Now, start from the beginning. What happened?" Bakoma didn't know where to start and kept on pleating the edge of her cloth while tears kept on rolling down her face. She couldn't look at her mother. Maame Adwoa took hold of her hand and asked urgently, "Bakoma, what is it? Don't kill me with this suspense. What has happened?"

Then Maame Adwoa remembered the report from Prince Prempeh about Prince Gyakari's treatment of her daughter the previous day and asked gently "Does this have anything to do with Prince Gyakari?" Bakoma looked up at her and nodded.

"Look, don't take what happened at the lower court seriously. I'm sure he is already ashamed of what he did. After all, the two of you have always been close and I'm sure he will never hurt you intentionally. Do you believe that?" Bakoma nodded and whispered in reply "Yes mother, but there's more..." She then got up and continued, "He came to apologise to me last night. But...but what he said is what is worrying me, mother."

Her mother got up as well and turned Bakoma to face her. "What did he say?"

"He said...he said...he loves me and ...wants to

marry me..."

"What? Are you sure he said that to you?" Bakoma nodded and this surprised Maame Adwoa who shaking her head said, "I don't understand this. I thought Prince Gyakari was wiser than this and I'm surprised that he of all people will make such...such an irresponsible statement. He knows he cannot marry you. In fact, a delegation has already been sent to the Chief of Kenkaase to ask for the hand of his daughter Princess Afrakoma in marriage to Prince Gyakari. You know that."

"I know but it seems as if he knows nothing about this delegation, why?"

"The queen wanted this to be secret for personal reasons. It's as if she is being forced to do it simply because it is the right thing to do but she's been reluctant to do so all these years and all of us are puzzled but she is not sharing her reasons with us. After all, Prince Gyakari is long past the age of having a betrothed."

Mother and daughter fell silent, each with her own thoughts. Then her mother turned again to her, "So what did you say to him?"

Bakoma raised her left wrist and as her mother saw the necklace, she really became alarmed.

"Ei Bakoma, you shouldn't have accepted it. It's not

right. What will the queen say to this?

Please don't do anything that will bring a scandal to this family," she pleaded.

"Oh mother, what am I to do? He insisted I wear it. As a matter of fact, he bound it on my wrist himself when I refused to wear it around my neck. I even reminded him of his responsibilities as the heir, but he wouldn't hear of it. You know how determined he is when he gets an idea into his head."

"Yes I know that very well, he's like a dog with a bone and I think the queen should know about this. It's better she knows you're an unwilling participant in this potential disaster before the news reaches her. Meanwhile, I'll advise you to remove this necklace from your wrist immediately because almost everybody can recognise who it belongs to. Do you hear me?"

She nodded and started to remove it while fresh tears began to fall again. Her mother became concerned and asked, "Bakoma, what is it now? Don't tell me you return his love?"

"Oh mother!" Bakoma exclaimed and threw her arms around her mother again sobbing. Maame Adwoa knew the implications of Prince Gyakari's token of his love for her daughter and felt very sad knowing that her daughter was in for a heart break.

Oh yes, any girl would easily fall in love with the handsome prince whose status even at that moment commanded a lot of respect from all and sundry. A very accomplished young man indeed, whose smile alone could set any woman's heart aflutter. But she never imagined that her own daughter would fall a victim to his numerous charms and for him to set a seal of such magnitude on any girl was indeed flattering. She didn't want heartbreak for Bakoma however, and wished for the first time in her life that she could walk up to Gyakari and give him a piece of her mind, but ... that was taboo. She also knew she had to help her daughter and tried to hush her up, taking her to her own room. Over here, she wiped her tears away and said, "Listen to me Bakoma. You know I'll do anything for you but this matter between you and the prince is beyond me. I wish there was something I could do. All I can say is that you must try very hard to forget him and if it's hard for you to do so at the palace, you can always move back home. I don't want to see you hurt. *Nsuo beto a, mframa di kan*. Your grieving now is a harbinger of worse things to come. I want better things for you. I don't want you to end up as his concubine. There are many able young men in this town who will be eager to marry you as their first wife, even among the other princes, so be patient. *Ntoboase ma nkunim di*, patience will surely bring you victory. Don't rush into anything with Prince Gyakari. I want your promise that you'll stay away from him."

Bakoma couldn't look at her mother and started to weep again. Maame Adwoa was indeed surprised seeing Bakoma so weepy for the first time in her life. She had never seen her lose control of herself because she was always so poised...so much in control of herself. But she knew she had to be firm for Bakoma's own sake so she decided to press for the promise.

"Bakoma, I am waiting for your promise else I'll have to inform your father."

"No, no mother, I promise. I promise you that I will stay away from him. Please don't tell Papa."

Maame Adwoa was satisfied with this because she knew Bakoma would never go back on her promise.

She therefore decided to go and see the queen all the same in order to make sure that her daughter was protected. The queen had been upset when Maame Adwoa informed her but she had refused to yield to Maame Adwoa's request that Bakoma move back home and had only promised to take care of the situation. The first thing she had done then was to give Bakoma her own maid with strict instructions never to leave her side no matter what; else she would personally answer to the queen. Bakoma had guessed and understood this gesture by the queen and had determined not to break her promise to her mother. This had not been easy for her since she and Gyakari always met at the dining table but Bakoma had always ignored the pleading in his eyes to meet him, and the queen had taken steps to ensure the two were never left alone, leading to Gyakari's frustrations.

Chapter Seven

This situation had continued for about two weeks and Prince Gyakari had become increasingly irritable and moody. None of his cousins dared to tease him now, afraid of sporting a black eye. He kept mainly to himself after their daily drills and went horseback riding afterwards, far from the palace and far away from Bakoma. His only companions were Agyei his body guard and Warrior, his horse. If it were possible, he would even stop dining with the family to avoid Bakoma but he knew his mother would be furious since she always insisted on prompt attendance.

On one such day, he had run his horse so hard that Agyei's inferior one had struggled to catch up with him. He finally caught up with his young lord at the riverside where he had stretched out on his back with his arms thrown across his eyes. Agyei knew that his lord was suffering but didn't know how to help him. This was a matter far beyond him. In the past, he had easily arranged a rendezvous with any girl who had taken his fancy but now, he even found it difficult to point his lord's attention towards any other girl and he knew the reason why. Bakoma.

Bakoma was technically beyond his lord's reach because he knew, as everyone did, that as the next chief of Nton, he should have no less than a princess as his first wife. He also knew that Bakoma's status at the palace would prevent her parents and even Nana Karikari, Gyakari's uncle and chief, from allowing her to be a second wife to the prince, no matter how wealthy or powerful. She couldn't be anyone's concubine either. Not even Prince Gyakari's. Her status was above that. She could easily be the queen's own child. This was the dilemma but Agyei knew that he had to do something soon before the gun powder they were all sitting on due to the prince's temperament exploded.

Therefore, he cautiously approached the prince and sat down beside him on the grass. Then a thought occurred to him as he chewed on a piece of grass.

"Nana, are you asleep?"

"No." The prince replied in a gruff voice without changing his position.

"I have an idea, that is if you will agree with me, of course."

"About what?" He spat out.

"About..about B-Bakoma.."

Prince Gyakari shot up like a bullet and stared hard at his bodyguard and confidante. Agyei moved back a space ready to take flight should the prince strike out but he was surprised when instead of hot angry words, the prince asked slowly and nonchalantly, "What about Bakoma?"

Agyei cleared his throat and replied, "Well I'm aware that she's been avoiding you and this…hasn't gone down well with you," he paused, looking at him.

"Well?" The prince urged impatiently.

"Well…so I'm thinking that if you can persuade Princess Boatemaa to your side, you may be able to see Bakoma alone…"

The prince continued to stare at Agyei as his statement sank in and then looked away in deep thought. He then stood up and started to pace with his bodyguard watching him. Then he stopped suddenly asking, "Agyei, how many pieces of cloth did I buy yesterday from the traders?"

"You bought two pieces of silk materials and two pieces of cloth, Nana."

The prince walked and knelt at Agyei's side and said, "As soon as we get back, you'll send one of the silk materials to Boatemaa from me and we'll take it from there. Let's go my friend." He ended with a smile and a pat on Agyei's back. He gave a whooping shout as he practically vaulted onto his horse. Agyei was relieved to see the prince in good spirits again and he prayed that their plan would work.

Back at the palace, Bakoma and Princess Boatemaa together with their maids were engaged in the game of *oware*. Bakoma who had often beaten anyone who played with her except Prince Gyakari, had kept on losing game after every game and this came as a surprise to the princess.

Finally, when she had lost the third game, the princess threw up her hands and said in exasperation, "What is wrong with you Bakoma? You're not concentrating!" Peeking at her friend closely she asked again, "What is the matter? Are you feeling unwell?" This was not plausible since Bakoma hardly fell ill. Bakoma stared hard at Boatemaa wondering whether to confide in her or not. She repressed the thought, rose up and walked to one of the windows in their living room. The princess watched her, cast an inquiring glance at Amponsah, Bakoma's maid, who in turn shrugged expressing ignorance. The princess walked up to her friend who at the time was eagerly soaking in the sight of Prince Gyakari who had just crossed the courtyard below the window. She wasn't even aware that the princess was right behind her till she heard a slight cough behind her. She sprung around in alarm hoping that she had not been caught. She met the inquiring look in Boatemaa's eyes and she flushed with guilt. They stared at one another for a moment and it was then Boatemaa put a word to that look in Bakoma's eyes. Yearning!

Realisation dawned on her so she decided to be sure. Turning towards the two maids who stood watching them, Princess Boatemaa signalled them to leave them alone. After the door closed after them, the princess took hold of Bakoma's right hand and pulled her along to her own bed.

"Bakoma, what is it?" she whispered. Bakoma didn't look up but kept staring at her hands, so her friend asked again, "What is it? You can trust me, you know. We're like sisters, she smiled as their eyes clashed and continued, "Can't you tell me what is bothering you?" Still, she received no response but grew alarmed when she saw the tears begin to gather like clouds in her friend's beautiful eyes. What? Bakoma crying? That will be the day! The princess took hold of Bakoma's hands and began to shake her.

"Ei, Bakoma please tell me. What is it? Has anyone here in the palace hurt you in anyway?"

Bakoma shook her head so Boatemaa decided to

take the bull by the horns and voiced her suspicions.

"Has ...has Gyakari done anything to...harm you?"

"No!" Bakoma cut in too quickly but she knew that there was no way she was going to get away from Boatemaa's persistent and probing questions and before she could say anything, Afrah, the princess's maid knocked and sought to enter. She entered with a parcel in her hands explaining that it was from Prince Gyakari to his sister. She also informed them that he wanted to see her afterwards. The princess was mad with joy upon seeing the brightly coloured silk material and exclaimed, "Look Bakoma, it's just like your own except the colour. Isn't it beautiful?" She got up and draped the material over her bosom.

"Yes Boatemaa, it is", replied Bakoma who suddenly remembered that she had never really sought confirmation from Gyakari about the one he had sent to her.

The princess broke into her thoughts with, "Bakoma, I'll be back. I want to know what this brother of mine wants by giving me this bribe," she ended chuckling as she went out followed by her maid.

Prince Gyakari was pacing in his living room while Agyei continued to watch him, praying earnestly that his plan would work.

"Gyakari? Oh there you are!" His sister exclaimed

bursting into the room smiling. "Thank you for the beautiful material. You were the one who sent the other one to Bakoma, right?" she asked cautiously looking at him through squinted eyes.

He paused for just a moment and nodded seeing his opportunity to strike while the iron was burning hot. He exchanged an anticipating look with Agyei and replied, "Actually, that's what I want to talk to you about."

"About the material…?

"No, no, about Bakoma." He watched his sister whose frown didn't quite surprise him.

"What about Bakoma?" she asked suspiciously.

Instead of responding right away, he took hold of his sister's hand and pulling her with him replied, "Come and sit beside me, Boatemaa." After they sat down, he went straight to the point. "Look, I need a favour from you…" He lifted his hands to stop her from speaking when he saw her lips begin to move guessing what she was going to say. "Just hear me out first Boatemaa. I had wanted to give you that gift anyway. I bought it especially for you so don't go having any ideas, do you hear me?" he asked, smiling.

His sister who was still puzzled at his words just nodded. He motioned her maid to leave the room. "Well, you see…" , he paused, got up, and not knowing where to begin, glanced at Agyei in frustration who urged him on with hand gestures. Boatemaa looked from Agyei to her brother and felt the situation really funny, seeing Gyakari tongue-tied for once. So she chuckled, "What is it with you and Bakoma? The two of you are behaving so strangely." She paused, a thought occurring to her sharp mind. "Is anything going on between you two, Gyakari?" He whirled on her suddenly trying to gauge her mood and when he saw the amused twinkle in her eyes, he sighed with relief and walked over to sit with her again.

"Look Boatemaa, you may not understand this but I love Bakoma," he paused and getting no response from her said, "Her mother and our mother know about this and are trying to stop us from seeing each other. That's why they gave her a maid." Understanding dawned on Boatemaa and he continued, "But I need to speak with her. It's very important to me. Please help me. Make a way for me to see her alone. Send her maid anywhere you want but please Boatemaa do this for me…" He ended in desperation, his forehead awash with perspiration.

Princess Boatemaa watched her brother. For him to plead and beg for a favour meant that the situation was grave indeed. She adored him and loving him as she did, she also wanted to protect him, even though

61

he was older than her.

"Do you know the consequences of your relationship with Bakoma, Gyakari?"

He stood up sighing, arms akimbo; he nodded and looking down at her replied, "I know but I'm prepared to take the risk. I'll deal with it when the time is right but right now, I've got to be sure of her because we have to leave for war against the Akyems in a few days and I…I may not return…"

She cut in, "Gyakari, I'll not hear of that nonsense. Apart from getting into trouble with mother if she finds out I've helped you, well…" Then she remembered Bakoma's listlessness and asked, "Does Bakoma return your affection?"

"Yes she does."

His sister stood up and said, "Well, I'll see what I can do…" but before she could finish her sentence, they heard the gong of summons for the warriors to see Nana Karikari go off. They

both looked at one another and Boatemaa decided at once. She took hold of his hands and said, "All right. Tonight. I'll take her to the lower court beside the mango tree. Be there." She immediately turned her back on him knowing that if she stayed any longer, she could change her mind for fear.

Chapter Eight

That night after supper, the Princess asked Bakoma to accompany her to the lower court but before then, she had asked the two maids to go back to their room to straighten things there and wait for their return. She took care to let them understand that they were not to go anywhere after that but wait for them upstairs when they finished their work.

Bakoma was puzzled about these requests even though it wasn't unusual for the princess to do such whenever she wanted to be alone. They talked about inconsequential things as they walked, watching the moon slide slowly across the skies as if drawing a curtain at the close of a play. Bakoma was so absorbed watching the moon that she walked ahead of Boatemaa without realising it. Then, Bakoma whose thoughts had been full of her lord, heard whispers and turned instantly to see Boatemaa walking away and Gyakari striding towards her.

Her heart leapt into her mouth as she heard a

rushing sound in her ears. She stood rooted to the spot like a frightened hare as Gyakari moved closer to her. He stopped a few paces from her and his eyes went straight to her left wrist which was clutching at her throat nervously.

"Where is my token?" he whispered. Her eyes broke away from his and she bowed her head without a reply. She felt, rather than saw him move closer. He lifted her chin up to face him. He could feel her tremble and saw the agony in her eyes. He immediately pulled her close, embracing her. She resisted a moment but gave in to the sobs that tore from her throat. He rocked her from side to side whispering words of endearment to her till she relented and relaxed. He set her away from him gently, took hold of her hand and led her to the seat under the mango tree. He pulled her close to his chest and they stayed like this for some time, savouring each other's presence; each drawing the needed strength from the other. Finally Gyakari spoke, "Bakoma," he called her in a whisper looking down at her and asked, "Do you love me?"

She didn't respond but her eyes began to fill with tears and swallowing hard, nodded.

"Then why aren't you wearing my token?"

"My mother asked me...to remove it."

"So where is it?"

"In my room, among my things."

When she paused he asked, "will you marry me?" She started in shock, easing away from him but his hand tightened around her shoulders, asking her again "Bakoma, will you marry me?" This time with an edge in his voice that brooked no arguments. She was frightened and knew she shouldn't break her promise to her mother and yet she also knew that she was in love with this man and her response surprised her.

"Yes, yes, O Gyakari!" as she threw her arms around him shaking and trembling from head to toe.

The prince was relieved to hear this and knew from that moment onward that at least he had won the first battle. As such, he determined that no one, not even his mother would be able to stop him from having Bakoma as his soul mate. He didn't know how he was going to achieve this. He only knew that he was going to do something; had to do something. He knew time was short to court her properly. He had to join the other warriors selected by their chief that afternoon to go to war in two days time. His plan was to set his seal properly on her against all odds but he also knew he needed her consent to do so. He didn't want to frighten her, all the same he wanted to make sure that Bakoma agreed to see him again on the morrow.

"I'm leaving for war, day after tomorrow."

"You? Why?"

He turned to her with a smile saying "But you've known all along that I'll have to go sometime,

don't you? *Eye me nkrabea*. Yes, that's my destiny."

"Yes I know, but so soon?"

Thinking desperately that she may lose him even before their love affair began, she began to

tremble. Gyakari also sensed a withdrawal in her and taking her face in his hands smiled saying,

"Don't worry, Bakoma. I'll come back. Having you waiting for me will help me to survive. Knowing that you are here and all mine will spur me to survive. You'll wait for me, won't you?"

"Yes…yes Gyakari. Forever," she whispered.

Then his lips descended on hers. He pulled her up with him, molding her slim but well-formed body against his strong solid one. They clung to each other desperately and when they came up for air he said, "Bakoma, oh Bakoma, I'll miss you. Wait for me, please?"

"I will Gyakari, no matter how long it takes," she pledged, knowing that some of these wars could take months and months. "I'll miss you too."

He broke the embrace and taking hold of her shoulders asked, "Will you meet me here again tomorrow, same time?"

She hesitated for a moment not knowing how that will be but she gave her answer in the affirmative. They embraced again in joy then hand in hand, happy beyond description, walked back to the palace, secure in their love for each other. Agyei walked several paces behind them looking out for any intruders.

He failed to see an enemy within, who had been watching them. His suspicions confirmed, Prince Bonsu, Gyakari's cousin and the first son of the chief decided to act immediately. He wanted Bakoma as well with a desperation he had never imagined he had till he had seen them together under that mango tree tonight. Why should Gyakari have everything? The throne, and the most beautiful girl on earth. Why?

"No, I won't allow it!" he vowed. "I know she won't even take a second look at me with Gyakari around even if I ask her. But Gyakari won't have her either. I have to report what I've seen to father!" With this promise to himself, he left the area.

The next day, Nana Karikari sent for Opanin Asaase, Gyakari's father informing him of what his son Prince Bonsu had told him. It was therefore with a grave face that Prince Gyakari met his uncle and his father in the council room. For once, his body guard Agyei was asked to wait outside. This alarmed him and looking from one face to the other, sensed that his love for Bakoma was at issue here. He therefore geared himself for battle. Battle for his love, Bakoma. His uncle motioned him to sit down and clearing his throat began with,"Gyakari, as the heir to this Nton throne you're well aware of your responsibilities, are you not?"

"I am aware, Nana."

"Good. My nephew, our elders say that *Oba nyansa fo, yebu no be na yennka no asem*. You are a wise child who should be spoken to in proverbs. The heart of man will soar where it will. Any mere man will allow this to be so but those with courage will not yield to this because it will hinder the course of their destiny. But since *Onyame nkrabea nni nkwatibea nti*, your God-ordained destiny cannot be avoided. It is true that no man can fight the cause of true love and win but when you are a prince, you must always put the interest of the throne and family and your people first before any interest of the heart. That is why we always make sure that an heir is betrothed very early in life in order to ensure continuity of our traditions. Your parents and I have realised the mistake we've made by not attending to your betrothal early but that will soon be remedied. As we speak, we await response from Nana Poku, the Chief of Kenkaase for his consent to our request to betroth his daughter Princess Afrakoma to you."

This last statement made Prince Gyakari shoot up like a bullet from his chair and his response was suddenly stilled by his father's raised hand in caution. He looked wildly from his father to his uncle and his body shook from the force of his suppressed fury as he sat back down. A look passed between the two older men in a silent message that seemed to say "It seems his love for Bakoma is too deep already." However, Nana Karikari was determined to see the matter to its true conclusion and decided to ignore this drama.

"As I was saying, I have reason to believe that Nana Poku will agree to our request if his daughter is free due to the status and wealth anyone marrying you will acquire. Since you're to leave for the war front tomorrow, preparations for the betrothal ceremony will go on in your absence..."

Again the prince shot up from his chair and this time refused to sit down at the command of his father as he began to pace. His eyes were filled with suppressed rage but he knew that he couldn't say anything till his uncle has had his say. His uncle continued as if nothing had happened.

"We pray that you'll return safely. You are a strong warrior, one of the best in this town and it is time for you to go to war for the first time to test your strength. We believe you're ready for war. Your skills in handling all manner of weaponry is well known and your trainers have nothing but praise for you. *Nanso, obarima woyen no dom ano, na enye fie,* you have to go to the battle front to prove your manliness. We believe strongly that you will return safely."

His uncle paused, looked at him and then asked "Now, do you have anything to say?" He asked bearing in mind that indeed they had made a grave mistake in not betrothing him to a princess when he was very young. This was partly because a betrothal was always binding and doing it early prevented the one betrothed when grown, to break it knowing the consequences of doing so. It also prevented the one betrothed from rejecting the choice of his parents for obvious reasons.

Sensing Gyakari's mood made him sympathise with him, knowing that it wasn't the young prince's fault that he was in such a quandary yet…

Gyakari stopped pacing and faced them. He responded with respect bringing his emotions under great control as his upbringing and manner as the future chief demanded.

"Nana, thank you for the information. I'm also grateful for your interest in my welfare but now that you've brought up the subject of my marriage, there is something I would like you and father to know." He paused as he saw the look that passed between them and he became more determined to press his suit. He felt he had to do it realising that he could use their mistake against them. He reasoned that if they have admitted their mistake in not providing him with a betrothed, then they might as well allow him to choose whomever he wanted to marry. "At least they should consider it and make some concessions for me," he thought.

He spoke, "Fact is, I already have another…another girl in mind that I would like to marry," he paused gauging their response but he didn't receive any not knowing that they were already aware of the situation even though Bakoma's name had not come up.

"Go on," his father urged.

"She is …she is Bakoma. I love her." He pleaded breathlessly, but still receiving no response, he continued, "I realise the responsibility I have towards this town, my family and the people but like you said, 'the heart soars where it wills'. Because you failed to give me a betrothed, my heart has already soared where it will. Love has no law. Can't you please for once, allow love prevail over tradition?" He continued to plead. "I love Bakoma and no other. I want her as my mate and

71

not as a second wife or…or…concubine…"

"Hold on Gyakari!" his father barked in anger. "Do you realise what you're saying? *Akoko ntakra nyin a, etua tua ne honam mu.* No matter how old you think you are, you're still subject to us and our traditions. Yes, we admit our mistake but do you foresee the consequences? *Ammamere, yento ntwene,* so you cannot, I repeat, you cannot bend tradition to suit your own purposes. We have heard your request. *Akyekyedie se, obarima mfere adwane,* so if you have made any promises to Bakoma, it's not too late to rescind them. I love Bakoma as my own child and would have liked nothing better than for the two of you to marry but it's impossible and you know it. *Se Onyame ma wo yarie a, oma wo aduro.* God can help you overcome your love for her in time. So stop pleading like a woman. Be a man and take our decision as final and leave Bakoma alone because we will not even consider her as a second wife for you. You know that she deserves better. What will be her status as a second wife for you? Will you always want your first wife to determine when you should and should not see her or when she should and should not see you? You know your first wife as the princess has those privileges and I wouldn't want Bakoma's status to be reduced to that level. I love her as well and if you really love her as you claim, then you must do what I'm saying. Only a princess can be your first wife and nothing less.

Nokware mu nni abira. There's no deceit in truth. So act like a man. *Anibere a, enso gya.* Every situation has its appropriate solution. Let her go. Your famed courage is needed here in this matter more than ever before. Your duties come first. Know as from today that Bakoma is taboo to you. She's not a princess, so forget her. *Anoma bone na osei ne mmrebuo,* remember, it's only the wicked bird who destroys its own nest. There will be dire consequences from the gods if we allow you to have your way in this matter which we know can certainly bring destruction on all of us. Do you understand this, son?"

Prince Gyakari stood like a statue. His father's words had sent an ominous chill all over him. He felt as if he was sinking. How could Bakoma be lost to him? But he had to be strong. He has to let her go. But can he ever do that? These thoughts ran riot in his mind as he sat down like a zombie. He couldn't believe what he had just heard and yet it was true.

"*O Twediampon,* help me." He sent up a silent plea to God.

"Gyakari, Gyakari!" His uncle called out to him urgently.

"Gyakari, are you all right?" His father asked anxiously seeing his face contorted in agony. The prince turned slowly to them, nodding and staring through them as if they didn't exist. He wanted to make one more attempt to secure their favour. "But... but at least, I have to see her one more time" he thought.

"Nana, I have heard everything you have said to me. I...I will obey but...but I have one request to make. Can I please see Bakoma alone today, one more time before I leave for war tomorrow?" The uncle and his father looked at one another surprised at how easy everything had gone and gave their consent immediately thinking that indeed Gyakari had matured in his role as the heir.

After this, Gyakari left the council room quickly followed by his guard. He went straight for his horse and galloped at a furious pace out of the palace walls. He liked the feel of the cool rushing wind in his hair and over his body clothed only in a short smock. He needed to cool down immediately. He didn't want to think. He wanted to forget about everything that had taken place that morning. He wanted to disappear. He wouldn't want to live if not for his responsibilities. He couldn't let his family down either. Yet, he was hurting. Love hurts. Love is costly. Love is madness and yet man always dares to love. Why? *Odo ye wu*. Love, indeed, is death. Love is not rational, can never be rational because the mere definition defies rationality. If love was rational, then why does one continue to love someone even when that person is forever lost to them? Even when that person loves another? And at times, even when that person is married to another? It is also a profound fact that love is sown not in the power of the mind but in the power of the heart and at this point, Gyakari's love for Bakoma was in the heart. Had it been in his mind, he would have been able to rationalise it away, allowing his grave responsibilities as the heir apparent to overrule the situation. But alas... the poor prince.

Chapter Nine

Akua Bakoma heard the news later in the afternoon after the lunch Gyakari had failed to turn up for. She knew that if Gyakari would dare to incur the queen's wrath by failing to attend lunch, then it has to be something very grave. So she felt devastated when she also learnt about the ultimatum given Gyakari by Nana Karikari and Opanin Daase his father to leave her alone. She wept as if all hope was lost. Her world, as far as she was concerned was collapsing. Why wasn't she born a princess? Is she doomed to live without Gyakari? If she couldn't marry Gyakari, then no other man would do. She wept violently, throwing herself about on her bed and rolling from side to side. Amponsah, her maid, fearing she might hurt herself, ran to go and call Bakoma's mother, Maame Adwoa Dapaa.

Maame Adwoa's heart was breaking seeing her like this. She gathered Bakoma in her arms trying to soothe her but to no avail.

"Bakoma, Bakoma, you're still young. Don't lose hope yet, even though Gyakari is not the man for you. You can have your pick of any man you want, my child. *Onyame na owo basin fufuo ma no.* God will help and provide for you. Please stop crying and try very hard to forget Gyakari."

"Oh mother, it's hard...so hard. I love him. I can never love another. I know I am young and yet I know my heart. I do love him. I know I can... never stop loving him. No never. Oh what will I do?" she ended sobbing hysterically.

It was at this point that the queen entered and sat down quietly beside the bed. She shook her head upon seeing the tears on Maame Adwoa's face and the way she was holding Bakoma like a baby. Her heart was touched and yet there was nothing she could do... She laid a comforting hand on Bakoma whose sobs had turned to hiccups as she rocked in her mother's arms trying desperately to bring her emotions under control in front of the queen.

"Bakoma," the queen began to speak. "We are all at a loss as to how to help you. I'm really sorry that you have to go through this but if it's any consolation, you have our permission to see Gyakari tonight, if you wish..."

Bakoma turned to look at the queen and her beautiful eyes filled with misery and swollen from crying, smote the queen's heart. She saw Bakoma struggle to smile as she nodded and said

"Thank you Nana. I…I appreciate your kindness."

Meanwhile, the news had flashed throughout the palace about Prince Gyakari and Bakoma.

Many were the sighs of regret for the two, knowing the pain the two must be going through. It led one old woman to say, *Abofra ketewa bi te fikese bimu a, ma no due, na wahunu amane,* yes, one must pity on the child who lives in a big, rich home, for he is over-burdened with responsibilities.

But one person was happy— Prince Bonsu. Things were certainly going his way. He then decided right away to put plan two of his actions into gear. He approached his father, the chief, and requested for Bakoma's hand in marriage. The chief gave his consent but warned him to wait till he returned from the war. He also warned him not to make any advances towards Bakoma till after Gyakari's betrothal ceremony if he didn't want another war to break out inside the palace. Prince Bonsu therefore decided to bide his time at this wise counsel but he swore that he would not allow Gyakari to have her, ever.

That night, Prince Gyakari awaited Bakoma at the

lower court with apprehension. He didn't know what he was going to tell her but he knew that he could never let her go. He was well aware that he couldn't have her as a wife either, which brought to mind the adage that *asantrofie anomaa woho yi, wo kye noa, wakye musuo, wogyae no nso a , wagyae srade*. He couldn't bear the thought of Bakoma in the arms of another man. The picture filled him with rage. "No! She belongs to me. She is mine," he almost screamed out.

His mind raced with ideas. How could he bind her to himself? He discarded one thought after another. The only way was to make love to her. He wanted to be her first, her last and the best so that she would never forget him. There was no two ways about that. He just didn't want to be a distant memory to her. And yet he felt that this idea was too selfish. What if she got pregnant? He didn't want to shame her with an unwanted pregnancy either. He still knew he couldn't marry her now, not even as a second wife as his father had made it known to him that morning. Then what? "Oh God!" he groaned as he passed his hand over his face and sat down with his head in his hands. He was really in a fix.

It was in this posture that Bakoma found him. He jumped as he heard her footsteps. Her special fragrance of musk hit his senses like a mighty wave.

He reeled under its assault, leaning against the seat for support, opening his arms into which she ran. They clung to one another for all eternity, their hearts beating against each other's. Gyakari finally put her away from him and gently brushed his lips against hers. Her instant response moved him to crush her closer against his hard body as their kiss deepened. They finally broke apart and Gyakari led her to the seat as they continued to stare into each other's eyes, hers as wet as dew. They continued to stare at each other, each pair of eyes mirroring the misery of the other's. Then Bakoma broke into sobs. He pulled her onto his lap and cradled her like a baby, shushing her as his hands caressed her arms. He wanted her desperately and yet suppressed the desire coursing through him. No words passed between them, their hearts and bodies making all the speech they needed. The prince knew he had to say goodbye to her forever. As much as he wanted to make her his, his responsibilities as the heir forbade him to do so. Pain and anguish, the kind of which he had never experienced, coursed through him making him tremble. He would have wept aloud if he could but the adage always said *Barima nsu*, no, a man must not cry. Bakoma became alarmed, lifting up her head from his chest and looking at him.

"Gyakari, are you all right?"

He nodded and as he stared at her and finally said, "You know we … we must…part, don't you?"

She continued to stare at him knowing the implications of what he was saying yet unwilling to understand it.

"Yes, I know…tomorrow…"

"No Bakoma, for…forever," he added in a whisper. She began to tremble.

"But you promised…you promised me…" she began but he laid his finger on her lips saying

"Yes, I did but…but Bakoma, I am overwhelmed by my responsibilities. I…I don't know what to do…" She interrupted him by getting off his lap despite the sudden tightening of his arms around her body.

"Gyakari, I'll be the last person to…to make you shirk your responsibilities as the heir but I…I love you. What am I going to do?" She broke into fresh sobs. He quickly got up and pulled her into his arms knowing full well that he might never hold her again; might never be allowed to make her his. Even then, he knew he must release her but he couldn't. Bakoma broke the embrace and began to undo her cloth. Gyakari watched her as if in a dream. He knew it was taboo to have a woman before a war. He knew he must turn away, but he couldn't move. Unknown to him, Bakoma had made a conscious decision for him to make her his own, undeterred by all that she knew about tradition; by all that she had truly believed until the reality of his danger in going to war had intruded; until the realisation of what he had told her earlier that he couldn't have her penetrated her lovesick heart. She believed Gyakari was hers and her body demanded the fulfillment of that ownership despite the reality of society's censure. This time was hers and his and might never be again.

"Bakoma..." he whispered, his voice hoarse and agonised with need, with want, with pain.

"Yes Gyakari, make me yours, please. Don't deny us this chance..."

"Bakoma," he cried again in desperation seeking to fight through the maze of desire enveloping him and seeking to deliver them both from disaster but he was beyond conscious thought, beyond any remembrance of right and wrong. This was his Bakoma. His very own and it seemed he'd loved her forever. If loving her was wrong, then he never wanted to do the right thing. It was only the realisation that if he broke the taboo for young warriors going to war by sleeping with a woman, he may never live to see her again which was unendurable. This realisation immediately pumped tons of adrenalin of courage and restraint into to him to stop her from giving herself to him. He therefore willed his body back into control. He grabbed her shoulders, shaking her in desperation.

"Bakoma, please think! It's taboo to touch a woman that way before war. Do you want me to live? Do you want me to return from war? Then please, help me! Stop this madness. I'll be beyond salvation if you don't help me to overcome my desire and need for you right now."

Bakoma's body withdrew its craving for Gyakari as his words penetrated her love-filled, hazy mind. She gasped, arranged her cloth and threw her arms around his neck.

"Oh Gyakari, I can't bear to lose you. Please, please return to…to me," she pleaded as her eyes sought his in the faint moonlight. He wanted to promise to return to her but he knew he couldn't give her false hope so in an agonised voice said "Bakoma, I shall return…yes, but…but?"

"Not to me…right?" she cut in a whisper as she turned away from him. He strengthened his resolve not to touch her again because he knew he would be lost. He had to be strong for both of them and he loved her too much to make her hope, when there was none for them. Therefore he decided to end their brief new found love affair.

"Bakoma, you know I love you and will always love

you…but…but I have to do this. I…I have to set you free from any promises I've ever asked of you. I… want you to go on with your… life."

He paused from the pain of not receiving any response from her. He continued with urgency "I don't know how I can bear it but if… if you don't want me to die in battle, distracted by you and how I've…I've left you in pain, then please, turn around and wish me well. Knowing that you've forgiven me will go a long way to… to help me survive on the field of battle. Please Bakoma, please. Will you forgive me?" He paused as he saw her turn slowly to face him, tears streaming down her face. Her beautiful face was bathed in anguish. Two hearts were breaking; two lives were being torn apart…two worlds were collapsing and yet…

"Gyakari," Bakoma responded in a stronger voice surprising him. "I release you from..any promise you've ever made to… to me. I… I want you to survive, not for me alone but for you. This town needs you, my love, but know this…" she laid her right hand under her firm breast, "That this heart of mine will ever beat for you and only you, God bearing me witness. May he protect you always. God speed, my love." And with this last prayer, she turned abruptly and ran back to the palace.

84

Chapter Ten

The warriors had been gone for three weeks. The preparations for the betrothal ceremony for Gyakari was in full swing but the air of excitement expected at such functions was subdued at the palace because of Bakoma's presence. At one point, she had offered to move back to her parent's house but the queen would not hear of it. Good reports of various victories against their enemies trickled in frequently from the war front. Bakoma never stopped praying for her prince. She constantly commanded her heart to stop beating for Gyakari's love but to no avail.

Meanwhile, the parents of a rich successful trader, who had returned from the coast, had approached Bakoma's parents for her hand in marriage. Bakoma didn't know this yet but her parents had hesitated to inform her because of her situation with Gyakari till she had returned suddenly to her parents' house one evening to find a richly-clad family visiting their home. She had not noticed the young man at first. She had politely greeted them and sat down. But sensing that someone was observing her, she lifted her eyes to glance in the direction where the feeling was coming from to meet the most penetrating eyes she had ever seen. The man was tall and fair in complexion. He wore his cloth with an arrogance she had never seen before, not even on Prince Gyakari. He was not as tall as her prince she figured but he was indeed handsome. She noted his straight nose set in the middle of high cheek bones with a pleasant mouth which she realised at that moment had begun to smile with a questioning look as if asking whether she liked what she was seeing. It was then she realised that she had been staring. She quickly turned away to meet her parents' eyes on her. Her father, Elder Ntim, introduced the visitors and finally informed her of their intentions. She was shocked to hear of their mission and also realised that this was not the visitors' first visit to their home. Her mind was in a turmoil. Her heart rejected what her head was telling her. Her mind struggled to accept the finality of Prince Gyakari's words the last time they had met. A sliver of pain shot through her. She couldn't accept it. Gyakari was hers. She belonged to him and yet he had urged her to go on with her life. It was both the good upbringing she had and great self-control that prevented her from running out of there; instead, with great courage, she smiled at the visitors.

So she had left her parents house that evening, promising them to allow the young man Akwasi Bretuo, to visit her now and then but she had asked her parents later on not to formalise anything between them yet. Her mother had looked at her with understanding and had not questioned her even though her father had been surprised by the request. But because of his love for her, he had acquiesced. Bretuo's visits to Bakoma weren't as frequent as he would have liked but he had heard of Prince Gyakari's interest in her and wanted to move slowly so as not to frighten her away into another man's arms. His numerous gifts to her had never been used because Bakoma preferred the necklace Gyakari had given her some months back. One thing she had to acknowledge was Bretuo's knowledge of places far away to the coast. She loved the stories about the white men and their castles and was even impressed about his knowledge of the white man's language, which he offered to teach her. She also liked some of the white man's clothes that he wore at times. She thought he looked dashing in them and he offered to buy her dresses which the white women wore. Bakoma always enjoyed these discussions and a certain amount of rapport slowly developed between them but not the kind Bretuo would have liked. Yet, he decided to bide his time knowing that Prince Gyakari was standing between them. He also knew that since their betrothal had not been formalised, he couldn't even hold her as he would have liked. He knew Bakoma was beautiful, the kind of girl who haunted men's dreams, especially his own, but he regarded himself as a man of the world, cultured and polished; having seen how the white men wooed their women on the coast and was determined to do same. So he was always satisfied with a peck on her cheeks after their meetings without going any further.

Since Gyakari left for the war, it had been Bakoma's pastime to always retreat to the lower court in the evenings, her rendezvous with her prince. On one such occasion, Maame Adwoa Dapaa, her mother, had followed her there. She saw her daughter sitting alone, lost in her thoughts so much that she didn't notice her mother standing near her till she heard her voice.

"Bakoma," she called her softly and the girl jumped.

"Mother, what are you doing here?" Her mother smiled and sat down beside her, touching her shoulders saying, "Oh so I can't visit my own daughter anymore?"

"I'm sorry mother. That was a foolish question." Her mother laughed looking at her fondly.

"You have really matured into a very beautiful woman, Bakoma. I'm really proud of you. No wonder all the young men in this town want you as their wife."

"Oh mother," she protested, ducking her head in embarrassment.

"Well, isn't it true? But be careful because I sense that Bretuo will not tolerate any competition...not even from your prince, so make up your mind soon."

Bakoma sobered up immediately agreeing to what her mother had said. She herself had noticed that Bretuo was possessive of her and wished with all her heart that she could return his love. She appreciated his restraint in not touching her, behaving as a gentleman whenever he visited her.

"Look, don't mind me Bakoma. That's not why I came to see you. I just wanted us to talk, ok? I am very proud of you and even the queen can't stop praising you. Whoever thought that that cry baby of yester-years would turn out to be like a princess?"

Bakoma listening to her talk wished with all her being that she were a princess because it would have solved all her problems but she couldn't voice this out knowing her mother would be hurt. Her parents had been good to her and she loved them, so she kept quiet as they sat in silent companionship.

"Do you remember when we used to go to the farm

together?"

"Yes mother. It is strange that for the past few years, I've never been there with you. Perhaps we should do so soon. What do you think?" Bakoma asked in excitement.

"I miss those times too. Those were the years before you moved to the palace and I don't think the queen will allow it now but I'll see what I can do, all right? I remember when you were five years old and we had gone to the farm. You had this cocoa plant your father had given you to take care of. One day while you were taking care of it, you just disappeared while we were busy digging up some crops. We started searching all over the farm for you only to trace you to that cave on that hill beside the stream. Do you remember?"

"Oh yes, don't I ever! I became curious as I started strolling about then I remember I wanted to fetch water from the stream to go and water my cocoa plant when I saw this hole in the mountain. So I decided to go in and investigate. I had just entered when I heard your frantic calls." They laughed together as the mother remembered how Bakoma had peeked out from the cave's mouth.

Bakoma continued wistfully, "Here at the palace, all we do is play games like oware, go horseback riding, swimming and of course sitting daily at the feet of

Maame Ataa who teaches us about our history and etiquette. The etiquette lessons I like best are the way we're taught how to dress, how to talk and how to walk." She laughed, "I must say that at times, it amuses me because what am I going to use all these lessons meant for princesses for, mother?"

"Don't worry Bakoma, just learn as much as you can. You'll be able to use all the lessons in etiquette in your home when you marry Bretuo and move to the coast with him." Her mother responded light heartedly, seeking to encourage her daughter to turn her affections towards Bretuo. Bakoma had to pretend that her mother's last words had not put a damper on her spirits; she sought to change the subject.

"How about my cocoa plant?"

"It has grown now and we have harvested it a couple of times over the years." Bakoma's mind went down memory lane again and turning to her mother asked, "Do you remember that magician who passed through here when I was ten years old, just before I moved into the palace?"

"Hmm, I heard about him. What happened?"

"What you were never told was that Yaa Yaa and Gyamfi, Maame Afua Kobi's children and I went to watch the show. The man actually turned some pieces of paper I saw him put into his box into cooked rice and then pulled me out of the crowd and stuffed the rice into my mouth."

She laughed at her mother's look of surprise.

"What? Really, was it with some soup?" She asked in disbelief.

Bakoma laughed again and replied "No, no just white rice without soup. Oh, it was awful and Yaa Yaa and her brother teased me unmercifully for days. I couldn't tell whose ears to box first those days and I couldn't tell you too because you were so protective of me and I went without your permission." She smiled mischievously.

"Hmm Bakoma, the scrapes you got yourself into those days!" Maame Adwoa said shaking her head in remembrance. "In fact I was so relieved when you moved in here because I was always so afraid for you. Especially when you slipped out of my hands on market days. I was always so frantic looking for you. On one such day, I found you sitting beside Maame Akosua Amponsah behind the blacksmith's shed, eating roasted plantain. I was so angry at you that day but Akosua persuaded me not to beat you. You were so restless then."

"How old was I then, mother?"

"Hmm, about four I think. From that time, I decided never to take you to the market again."

"Oh mother, so that's it! You worry too much!" She laughed and hugged her. Her mother thought about how she found her as a baby and never ever wanted to lose her.

"I love you Bakoma. You are my only child and I don't want anything bad to happen to you."

She looked at her mother sensing that there was something more behind her words. She bit her lips, a habit she exhibited whenever she was nervous and asked, "Mother, is something wrong?"

Maame Adwoa sighed and replied, "You have not shown any real interest in Bretuo's request. It's been over a month now, daughter. He can't wait forever you know, he is a very busy trader. In fact, he's been patient enough, don't you think, hmm?" Bakoma stood up and picked up a dry twig twisting it in her hands. Her mother watched her for a moment and continued with "Bakoma, I know you're thinking of Gyakari but it's not right. Fact is, if Gyakari encouraged you in anyway, it wasn't wise at all for him to do so as our future chief…"

"Mother!" Bakoma cut in quickly, her eyes flashing and revealing the temper she rarely showed.

"Gyakari hasn't encouraged me in anyway," and then turning away to hide her pain, continued, "I'm the one who can't forget him." She ended miserably. "Actually before he left, he asked me to forget him…and…and move on with my life but it's so…hard."

"Bakoma, my baby," Her mother got up to embrace her knowing the futility of her daughter's feelings for the heir to the throne. "Come. Sit down with me. Look, I know this is hard for you but preparations are completed towards Gyakari's betrothal to Princess Afrakoma. Unless a miracle happens, there's nothing you nor I or even Gyakari can do to stop it. My child, forget the prince. Do your best and turn your attentions to Bretuo. I can see that he cares for you very much and would also love you. He is wealthy and as handsome as Gyakari but unlike Gyakari, he is free to do whatever he wants. He could even take you to the coast to go and see all those white people he often talks about. You will be able to travel all over the world. What more can you want in a man?"

"Mother, I don't love Bretuo, that is the difference. I respect him and his worldly ways and I wish I could love him but I can't. And I…I don't want to encourage anything that…that may not lead anywhere." She answered in anguish. Her mother cupped her face in her hands saying, "Bakoma, listen to me. I have never ever pushed you into doing anything you didn't want to do but this time I have to. *Obaatan na onim nea neba bedie.* I have to, for it's only a loving mother who knows what is right for her baby. I know what is right for you and you must trust me in this. You will be hurt if you persist in the way you're going. Learn to love another. *Nkrabea nyinaa nse*; destinies do differ. You have yours and so does Gyakari. He is doing what has been destined for him and so must you. Gyakari may not be your destiny but Bretuo can be; but you could lose Bretuo as well if you don't give him a little encouragement. I repeat urgently to you, learn to love another, knowing that Bretuo loves you should generate something in your heart for him. Gyakari is lost to you, my child."Bakoma removed her head from her mother's hands with a sharp cry, startling her mother as she broke into sobs. Maame Adwoa hugged her, sensing the pain she was going through because of her words but she knew that for a wound to heal, one must cauterise it. She knew Bakoma would have more pain when Princess Afrakoma eventually came down to join Prince Gyakari so she was desperate to push her daughter's mind towards another. She allowed her to cry on her shoulders for a while as Bakoma struggled to come to terms with her fate. But it was this heart-to-heart talk with her mother that made Bakoma resolve to encourage Akwasi Bretuo's advances and their betrothal date was set.

Chapter Eleven

After two and half months at the battlefront, the warriors returned. Prince Gyakari returned. Those at the palace had received news of their impending return from runners who had brought the report. The palace buzzed with activity. Three cows as well as goats and deer had been slaughtered for food: soups, stews, khebabs, the traditional *bosoa* sausages, as well as the occasional *ekyim*. Large pots of palm wine were cooling under the trees in the upper court where stools and chairs had been arranged for the celebration of the warriors' victorious return. Among the drinks to be served were large quantities of rum brought from the coast. That morning, Princess Boatemaa and Akua Bakoma had their hair braided; Bakoma had beads braided into her long hair. By afternoon, they had donned their two piece silk outfits. Bakoma looked ravishing in the aquamarine silk Gyakari had given to her. Only the crease between her eyebrows and the constant biting of her lower lips revealed her state of nervousness about Gyakari's return. She knew he had survived the war, else they would have heard of his death before this time. She had not been able to sleep well that night waking up from one dream to another about her warrior prince. She had relived the number of times she had spent in his strong arms and despite the warnings in her mind about the futility of everything, her heart stubbornly clung to her love for Prince Gyakari. The chief and his family, the queen and her family, as well as the elders and their family members, with a great number of the people of Nton were in holiday mood. No one went to the farm and every usual business was suspended. Members of the royal household as well as elders had all gathered at the upper court awaiting the return of the warriors.

All the drums were silent here as the drummers waited anxiously to receive the drum signal from the outskirts of the town which would signal the arrival of the warriors. There was a feeling of anticipation in the air.

"Oh, this waiting is killing me, Bakoma. I hate this." Princess Boatemaa said to her friend. Her companion turned to look at her smiling and teased, "Well, should we expect a lover among the returning warriors?"

Boatemaa nudged her friend as they both burst out laughing.

"Come off it Bakoma. If I had, wouldn't you know, hmm?" Then turning to her friend asked "Where is Bretuo?"

Bakoma shrugged, replying, "Somewhere among the crowd, I guess," she replied as she looked down at her slippers. But Boatemaa would not be put off so easily. "Look Bakoma, you've been very quiet about Bretuo. You've always changed the subject whenever I've asked you about him, why? The man loves you. I can tell from the way he looks at you. His numerous gifts to you are also declaring his love for you, so what is the problem?"

Bakoma shrugged again without responding.

"It is still Gyakari, isn't it? No, no don't say anything," Boatemaa lifted her hand to stop any interruption; she went on, "I am sorry I have to say this now because I know you can't run away from here as you usually do every time the subject matter comes up. I am concerned about you but you're always dodging me. I hear how you moan and whisper Gyakari's name in your dreams at night…" she paused when Bakoma turned to look at her in alarm. "Yes Bakoma, you've been doing that since he left but…but I have just kept quiet. One thing I know is that whatever happens between you and my brother, you will always be my sister and dearest friend."

Bakoma's eyes filled with tears as they turned in one accord to embrace. They were suddenly brought to their senses by shouts of war songs and drums. The drummers inside the palace responded with their own drums and everyone, especially the women in white cloths began to wave their white scarves and cloths, singing and dancing. The atmosphere was charged under the hot sun. People had started to surge through the palace gates as the dancing and drumming from outside the palace walls got closer.

"*Atadwe, ene yeate de nne, atadwe, ene yeate de nne*"

"We have heard great news today; we have heard good news today!"

The people sang and danced into the courtyard leading the warriors in. Then the warriors, each with a white strip of cloth tied to their heads poured through the palace gates led by Prince Gyakari. Wild cheers broke out as women removed their scarves and tossed them into the air. Prince Gyakari was surrounded by his guards but he was suddenly lifted up shoulder high as he waved the gun and the spear in each hand to acknowledge the cheers from the crowd.

Bakoma heard a roar like wind in her ears. She was strung as tight as a drum, her heart beating like a gong in her chest. She couldn't join in the dancing and the movement around her as her eyes only sought out her love. Prince Gyakari had also dreaded the meeting. He had thought about her both day and night during their return march home. His eyes began to search for her as soon as they neared the place where his family had gathered hoping that she would be there. Then he found her standing still. Their eyes clashed and once more heat surged through him. He knew he was trapped again. He knew he had to do something. But… had she waited for him? He knew he had released her from any promise she had made to him, but oh, how he wished she'd waited. His musings were interrupted when he realised that he was being set down and being urged to receive the blessings of his uncle and his mother the queen.

Akwasi Bretuo, standing where Bakoma could not see him, had watched all this with dread hoping that Bakoma would have forgotten her prince but upon seeing her reactions towards Prince Gyakari, concluded that Bakoma's heart was still lost to the prince. Yet he was still willing to make her his own wife. He wondered whether Bakoma had already given her virtue to the prince. He wouldn't think about that now, but vowed that no matter what, Bakoma would eventually be his. He vowed to take her far away to the coast after their marriage so she would forget the prince. With these thoughts in his mind, he left the palace.

The jubilation culminated in a joyous feast of both plantain and yam *fufu* with different types of soup: palm nut, groundnut, and light soup; rice and stew, and assorted khebabs. Palm wine and rum had flowed like rivers and many were those who had left the palace with leftovers of the feast.

◆ ◆ ◆

Bakoma listened quietly to the stories of war narrated by Princes Gyakari, Osei, Bonsu and Kyeretwie as they feasted.

"It really takes great strategy to win a war!" exclaimed Gyakari. "It never failed to amaze me how skillfully the *twafoo*, the advance guard, who were almost always hidden in trees, swooped down on the enemy whenever we were attacked!"

"Yes Gyakari,'" agreed Prince Bonsu. "It was always so exciting. I never thought going to war would be so exciting. In fact, what surprised me most was their prowess. There were times I wished that I was among them and not among the *adonten*, the main body of the army," added Prince Bonsu.

"Well son," his father the chief said "No royal family member can be in that group because of the great risk involved. These people you're talking about are trained and highly skilled warriors and very good at what they do. You have to be an experienced warrior to become part of them. More often than not, the success of any war depends on them because they and the *nkwansrafoo*, the body of scouts have to map out the layout of the enemy and to gauge their strength. If they fail to do this properly, the whole army could be doomed. Another thing you have to know is that during the war, all the royals have to be protected because even if one of you is captured, that could also spell the end of the war." Prince Prempeh, the youngest of the queen's children listened to all these stories wide eyed, wondering when it would be his turn to go to war. Apart from a cut across the thigh of Prince Bonsu, none of the royal warriors had sustained any injuries.

The lovers' eyes clashed several times during which Bakoma was always the first to turn away. Gyakari wondered whether he could see her that night but he cancelled the thought knowing that he had lost that right. The next day though, he became more determined to see her when Prince Bonsu, wanting to torture him, had informed him of Bakoma's impending betrothal to another man.

The news had hit Gyakari like a mighty blow in his guts. If not that he was seated at the time of the news, drying himself with a towel after their morning weaponry exercises, he believed he would have collapsed. He couldn't bear it. Thoughts of Bakoma in another man's arms ran riot through his mind all the way to his chambers. Had she...had she given in to this man? No! He couldn't think about that.

"No, Bakoma is mine. Mine alone and I will not..."

"Will not what?" interrupted a voice belonging to his brother Prince Osei who had just entered the chambers they shared to hear his brother's loud musings. Prince Gyakari whirled on his brother, unconscious that he had spoken his thoughts aloud. Prince Osei defied his brother's volatile temper and with arms akimbo chided him softly, "Gyakari, you're being selfish, do you know that?"

"Selfish? What do you mean by that?" he asked advancing menacingly on his younger brother who continued to stand his ground.

"You...you know you can't have Bakoma. You are as good as betrothed from what I'm hearing to Princess Afrakoma. So let Bakoma go. Free her."

Gyakari roared, "Osei, shut up! Who are you to order me to let her go? Bakoma is mine! She has always been and will forever be."

His younger brother replied with equal vehemence, "Gyakari, come to your senses. You are heir to the throne, you can't…"

"Can't what? I could marry her…"

"But not as your mate," Osei cut him off. "And will Bakoma accept that, heh? Gyakari, do you really believe that Bakoma will accept that?" Prince Osei continued to reason with his brother, pleading with him, even though he knew the pain his brother was going through. "Think Gyakari! There's more at stake here. I know you used to withdraw into yourself during the war after every skirmish with the Akyems. You were always vulnerable during those moments and I had to personally make sure that the guards and Agyei never left your side. You could have been killed, you know? I was so worried about you." He paused and went to sit beside his brother on his bed where he had retreated to.

"Gyakari, I know how much you care for her but think about her now, aside from yourself.

Would you imprison Bakoma to yourself as a second wife when she could have any noble man she wants, ha? Set her free, Gyakari. Let her go, for goodness sake. If you love her as you say, then let her go."

He paused when Gyakari stood up abruptly and walked to the window. He had heard that chorus before "Let her go, if you love her" but he couldn't see how. Prince Osei watched him for sometime wondering whether his words had sunk into his brother's thick skull. Seeing the struggle his brother was going through, his heart went out to him and he got up, walked slowly to his side clasping his shoulders with one arm and for the first time in many years, felt his brother Gyakari tremble with weeping. He remained silent watching him and empathising with him for the great responsibility his brother carried which had robbed him of his great love. They stood like this for some time and then Gyakari turned around, patted his brother and walked out of their room without a word. He was followed by Agyei who had witnessed the scene with awe. Gyakari weeping? He couldn't believe it. Agyei was happy that he was not royalty and could have any woman he wanted but his heart bled for his young lord. Agyei followed his lord as they went horseback riding, far into the woods. Gyakari grieved silently and failed to see that it was even time for supper. Agyei didn't want to interrupt him and watched and guarded him silently from a distance because he wouldn't intrude on his lord's moment of grief.

When it was almost dark, they returned to the palace and Gyakari's feet carried him automatically to the lower court where another visitor was already seated. Bakoma. He stopped short, surprised, not knowing what to do, whether to turn back or continue towards her. He turned around to find Agyei behind him; he dismissed him.

Chapter Twelve

Bakoma had quickly gone to change into another cloth after the supper which Gyakari had again failed to attend. She had dismissed her maid and had sought refuge at the lower court to go and sort out her feelings. She had realised with fresh anguish that Prince Gyakari meant everything to her. She had sobbed and prayed for a miracle that would change her situation because she believed that anything less than that had the potential to turn her into a spinster forever; the other alternative being a loveless marriage which as far as she was concerned, was worse than death. Even though Bretuo was an able substitute, she didn't want him in her life. She couldn't bear the thought of sharing Gyakari with anybody else, not even a princess.

"Oh Gyakari, my love. *Nkrabea ni*! Is this destiny? What will I do without you?" She screamed to herself. She jumped as she felt his hands on her shoulders. She could recognise that touch even in her dreams.

The way it made her feel. When she turned to look up at him, his intense gaze on her confirmed to her that he had overheard her cry of anguish. She continued to stare at him as he sat down beside her.

Then they were in each other's arms. Moulding one another to themselves as lips met and tongues warred with each other. Theirs was a hopeless cause and they clung to one another in desperation. Finally after a while of silent communication of souls, hearts and bodies, Gyakari asked the question which had been burning in his heart since that morning. He set her away from him and looking searchingly at her, as if to identify the other man's seal on her asked, "Do you ... care for this other man, Bakoma?"

Her eyes widened with surprise. "Who...how did you...who told you?" She whispered the questions in confusion.

He waved her questions aside by repeating his question. "Do you care for this other man? Tell me. I want to know!" He asked in a whisper dreading the answer at the same time.

She hesitated for a moment and then replied "No... no Gyakari. I don't think I can ever care for another as I care about you."

He was still not satisfied, somehow rankled that she didn't waste any time finding a replacement for him, so he asked again "Are you sure about that? It seems you wasted no time finding a...a replacement for me." There, the dreadful words were out at last.

Bakoma pulled away from him and flushed, "Gyakari! That's not fair!" She looked so ravishing in her anger that he was not listening to her protests and pulled her against him once more wishing he could hold her forever but Bakoma pulled away and said,

"Your betrothal is in a week, Gyakari. I can't stop you. You asked me to go on with my life.

That's why I gave in to Bretuo..."

He brusquely interrupted her with "Is that his name, this man?" He took hold of her shoulders. Bakoma looked up at him and nodded, swallowing air in anxiety because everyone had learnt to fear this particular tone Gyakari uses whenever he's about to attack anyone who may have displeased him.

"Did he... has he touched you in anyway?" he asked with controlled anger knowing and dreading that a betrothal or even a hint of it between two people gave the man involved the right and approval to regard the woman as a wife in every way.

Sensing what Gyakari must have been thinking, Bakoma moved quickly to reassure him, though she resented his questions and he knew it wasn't her fault but she loved him and didn't want him to suffer.

"No Gyakari," but he would not even allow her to finish and rushed in with another question,

"Has he ever kissed you?"

Bakoma got up quickly leaving his embrace but Gyakari quickly followed suit pulling her around to face him, trying very hard to control his anger.

"Bakoma, answer…me!" he asked in staccato.

She began to tremble. Fearing his rage and hating herself for her weakness, she charged at him angrily, "How dare you question me like this when you are the one who is as good as married? Did you not ask me to get on with my life? What did you expect me to do?" She spat out these questions at him like bullets. "You have no right, no right to ask me that Gyakari."

"No right?" he roared as he interrupted her but she didn't flinch; she was very angry now.

"Yes, none whatsoever! You asked me to get on with my life. You're the one about to be engaged to another! How do you think I feel? And…and…"

"And what Bakoma?" Hoping that at least she was still his.

"Gyakari, leave me alone!" She charged removing his hands from the shoulders he was holding in his rage.

"No! I won't! Do you hear me? You are mine Bakoma. You have always been mine!" he roared and

Bakoma burst into tears.

"Oh God, what do you want me to do?" But her tears this time didn't gain her any sympathy with him. He was relentless in his pain and frustration. He knew he was hurting her but he couldn't help himself. He needed to know before he went crazy with jealousy.

"Bakoma, has he ever…kissed you?"

She looked up at him and nodded. He had guessed so from Bakoma's reactions yet he had hoped somehow that it wouldn't be true. He felt chilled and couldn't believe his ears. Bakoma in another man's arms when he had forsaken all others for her? He turned abruptly and left her sobbing. She knew then that she had to leave the palace because she couldn't bear to see Gyakari again. She loved him, yes but she wouldn't allow him to torture her day and night by his accusations.

She had done no wrong and wouldn't accept any punishment Gyakari may devise to torment her with. She learnt from that moment that she would never allow any man, not even a prince to dominate her even though their culture demanded it. She vowed to herself that she would never respond ever again to the whims of any man. So it was that very early the next day, the third day after the warriors had returned, Maame Adwoa got up to find her daughter and her maid at their gates. She embraced her and took her to her old room, the one she was using before moving to the palace. Her mother didn't ask any questions and seeing she needed to be alone, went out of the room taking Amponsah with her. It was at breakfast that morning when Bakoma's presence was missed that the queen asked about her.

Princess Boatemaa informed her mother and all the others that Akua Bakoma had moved back to her parents' home. Everyone was shocked, especially Prince Gyakari. He stopped eating, wiped his mouth with the towel provided and left the dining room unceremoniously. The queen was shocked to hear of Bakoma's move. As upset as she was with Gyakari leaving the table without permission, she also sympathised with his situation and decided not to query him. He had not slept throughout the night; torturing himself with all sorts of things concerning Bakoma and her man. He had keened in agony but he knew then that he couldn't go against tradition, so early that same morning, Gyakari had come to terms with Bakoma's loss to him and in his own way, said goodbye to his first love. But hearing of Bakoma's return to her parent's house had cut him to the quick because he knew that as from that day, Bakoma's presence in the palace would become very scarce.

Even though he knew that would be for the best, he still couldn't bear the thought of not seeing her daily. After this incident, feverish preparations towards Prince Gyakari's betrothal ceremony to Princess Afrakoma were put into high gear and ten days after the warriors returned from the war front, the D-Day finally arrived.

Bakoma had come to terms with Gyakari's betrothal to another and after much pressure from Bretuo, had given in that their own betrothal ceremony would take place a week after the prince's.

All this while, Gyakari had hardly seen Bakoma except from a distance but he had done his own investigations to discover the man he was losing Bakoma to. He had consoled himself with this knowledge that at least Bretuo had all the resources to treat Bakoma well and give her a good life. After this realisation, he had reluctantly released her from his life but not from his heart and had set his mind towards his own betrothal. So on this day in October, all was set and even Bakoma wore a new piece of silk material made with little black roses on a beige background, a gift from Bretuo. Her parents had spared no expense to make her look regal, even Princess Boatemaa couldn't help but be a little envious of her friend. Visitors from far and near had been arriving at Nton for the past few days and were still arriving on this day.

The entourage of the representative of the Atagyahene, Nana Osei Appiah had arrived from as far away as Kubease, led by Prince Kwame Boakye, the previous day. On this day, as Prince Boakye and his linguist, Opanin Kofi Basa took a tour of the palace, they came across Bakoma with her maid, crossing the courtyard behind the dining room.

Opanin Basa stopped short; he stood rooted to the spot as he stared hard at her. Prince Boakye turned to find out what had attracted the eyes of the old man.

"What is it, Opanin or have you found another beautiful young woman for your house?" the Prince teased.

"Look at her," pointing at Bakoma as he whispered. "Doesn't she look like someone we know?" Prince Boakye turned his full attention towards the girl.

"Hmm, she does look like my sister, Princess Bensuaa."

"That is it! The resemblance between this girl and the princess back home is remarkable! One might even think they were twins!" Then turning to his young lord said, "She resembles your late mother too, you know?"

"Really? Well, I was very young when she died

during the war of 1698, so…"

The older man paused again then said, "I'm very much interested in finding out who her parents are," he said thoughtfully.

"Why, Opanin, are you interested in this particular girl?" he asked laughing.

"Eh, no not really, not that way but it will be interesting to find out that's all."

The prince dismissed this incident from his mind but not the linguist. As soon as he got the opportunity, he requested to see Nana Karikari and with due respect inquired about the girl. His probing questions prompted Nana Karikari to send for Queen Gyamfua and a few elders. It was then that they were informed of how a baby princess from Kubease had been plucked from her dead mother's arms at exactly around the same time that Bakoma was discovered. This piece of information caused a lot of consternation among them and they demanded more proof.

"Well Nana and elders, *Okraman na obu be se, adekesee nyera*, no valuable thing ever got lost.

The royals of Kubease have a dark mark shaped like the heart behind their thighs. Every single one of them, male and female has this mark. Nana, you may call Prince Boakye and verify what I am saying."

"Does the prince know that you're inquiring about

this girl?" the queen asked.

"No, Nana but during our walk this morning when we came across her, even the prince admitted to the resemblance of this Bakoma to his sister Princess Bensuaa."

A murmur went up among those gathered. Joy in the queen's heart soared. Could it be that Bakoma, their Bakoma, was the lost child? If so, then she is a princess and Gyakari...her mind flew towards her son.

"Oh my God, Gyakari can marry her," she thought feverishly. "I have to do something quickly." With this resolve, she asked to send for Bakoma's parents.

◆ ◆ ◆

Elder Ntim and Maame Adwoa arrived with haste to the urgent summons. The news was broken to them. Maame Adwoa nearly fainted when she realised that the description of the mark in question was the same as the one Bakoma had. The elders rushed to her aid as she burst into wailing and confirming Bakoma's birth mark at the same time. There was uproar. Opanin Basa quickly sent for his prince. Prince Boakye came in and showed them the mark. He was clearly stunned. After all these years to finally meet his long lost sister that everyone believed was dead. Incredible! Unbelievable! Then he began to pace, remembering the story of how their father, Krotweamansa Takyi Panin II, had followed the Atagyahene to war and since the war captains and commanders could take their women with them, he had taken their mother, Princess Yaa Agyeiwaa and his baby sister, Princess Adutwumwaa, along. But unfortunately, an enemy had broken through their ranks and had attacked his mother, stealing the baby after killing her. Since then, they had not heard of their baby sister again.

Everyone had forgotten that a ceremony was to take place that afternoon while awaiting the arrival of Princess Afrakoma and her entourage from Kenkaase. Then a messenger arrived from Kenkaase to announce the death of Nana Poku, Princess Afrakoma's father and requested a postponement of the ceremony. The queen heaved a sigh of relief thinking, "Could this be fate?" Then she remembered that Bakoma had to be informed; she also had to confirm the mark on her as the final proof to the claims of the visitors from Kubease.

Chapter Thirteen

Bakoma had been upstairs in the room which she had shared with Princess Boatemaa when the summons came. They had been discussing the postponement of the betrothal ceremony which had come as great relief to her but nothing, nothing had prepared her for what she was about to hear later on. She entered the council room to find everyone present, including some strangers. Her bearing, poise and beauty struck all present that indeed, Bakoma could be a princess. The lost child. After greeting everyone, she was asked the most intimate question she would ever have to answer in public. She replied that she had a mark and described the mark. Everyone was stunned. She was finally persuaded to lift up the cloth at her back to reveal her beautiful straight legs with the mark. "*Ah, ɔkɔtɔ nwo anoma ampa!*" Opanin Basa, the linguist from Kubease exclaimed with joy, indeed, the crab could never spawn a bird! Then he continued with "Hmm, *wokyere akokɔ batan a, wosesa ne mma kwa*; indeed, when the hen is captured, her chicks are always fair game for others. If the mother had not been killed, I'm quite sure they would never have been able to steal her baby. Ei, destiny, hmmm!"

Everyone was excited and moved by this discovery. Bakoma couldn't understand what was going on especially when she found herself embraced by a total stranger. Her brother, Prince Kwame Boakye. She cried out in alarm and pushing away from him saw tears in the eyes of the stranger. She couldn't understand what was happening. She was perplexed, looking from one person to the other, and seeing her mother weeping uncontrollably, ran to her side.

"Mother, mother what is wrong?" she asked anxiously. The woman she had known for sixteen years turned to her, embraced her and continued weeping. It was then Queen Gyamfuaa called Bakoma to her side where she gently broke the news of her royal birth to her. She would have collapsed if not for the quick intervention of the guards. She was in shock. She gulped for air as she was led to a seat beside the queen. She was given water mixed with a little rum to revive her. What? A princess? Maame Adwoa and Opanin Ntim not her real parents? She rose up still in shock and walked slowly up to the man they claimed was her brother, Prince Boakye. She searched his face and asked in a whisper "Are you sure?" He smiled at her and replied,

"Yes, no doubt about it. You are my sister, you were named Princess Adutwumwaa."

Bakoma shook her head slowly and walked back to Maame Adwoa. She knelt beside the woman she had always known as her mother, threw her arms around her and broke into uncontrollable sobs. Almost every eye was wet with tears. Princess Boatemaa, who had been sent for by her the queen walked up to Bakoma and touching her shoulders, peeled her away from Maame Adwoa's arms and took her upstairs to their room.

Plans had been made to send a message to inform Nana Takyi Panin II of his child's discovery. Meanwhile, news had flashed through the town of Nton about Bakoma's parentage. The populace was reeling with shock and couldn't believe what was happening to their royal family. The betrothal postponed! Bakoma, a lost princess! Wonders will never cease! While some received the news with shock and how they were about to lose their feast for that day, others confirmed their belief that Bakoma had always behaved like a princess.

Odehyie, yempae ampa! A person of royal blood

doesn't need to be proclaimed, it always shows. Maame Adwoa's friends had come to take her home; she was inconsolable, she was going to lose Bakoma, her only child.

"*Sika nko adidi nsan mma kwa*, Adwoa," consoled one of her friends Maame Panin "I believe strongly that whatever you have sown into Bakoma's life will return to you tenfold, if not one hundred fold. You wait and see."

"Yes Adwoa, take heart," cried Afua Kobi. "We have heard that Bakoma's mother died the day she was stolen so you are still her mother!" she exclaimed and hugged her friend.

"Afua has really made a valid point now look at it this way," another of her friends, Akosua Amponsah smiled widely like the cat who got the cream. "If Bakoma is a princess, then our own Prince Gyakari can marry her now!" She ended triumphantly. All the others clapped in excitement as this realisation dawned on them.

"And Adwoa, you know what that means, don't you?" asked Maame Panin. "Bakoma will always live in this town!" Everyone began to clap as they danced around their friend, now a princess' mother. All Adwoa kept on saying was, "Oh God thank you. *Awurade meda woase ooo.*"

Prince Gyakari and his brothers heard the news much later because they had been out horse riding. When he heard the news on their return to the palace, Gyakari had shot up like a bull still not really realising the implications of Bakoma's birth. Prince Osei had run to hug his older brother congratulating him of his good fortune, which others present, including his cousins had not realised as well.

"Good fortune, Osei?" Gyakari asked not comprehending Osei's statement.

"Yes Gyakari! Don't you see now? Bakoma is a true princess from one of the most powerful families in Asante kingdom. My, she even outranks you, if you ask me." Prince Osei ended with enthusiasm, overjoyed for his brother. The others reacted to this revelation with cheers, except Prince Bonsu, who now knew he couldn't stop Gyakari his cousin from marrying Bakoma. As this revelation sank into his consciousness, Gyakari sat down heavily, open-mouthed. All he could utter was, "Oh God, God, God."

Then he ran out, followed by Agyei, straight to the council room where his mother, his uncle and the two visitors from Kubease he had met the previous day were still discussing the day's events. He stopped running as soon as he saw them and walked sedately into the room. His inquiring eyes darted to his mother, who, understanding his silent query, nodded with a smile.

Then the queen introduced Gyakari again to them and informed them of her son's interest in Bakoma which because of tradition, he had been forced to set aside. Prince Boakye got up, walked to Prince Gyakari and said, "You will be a welcome brother-in-law, Gyakari." They shook hands. Prince Gyakari couldn't contain his joy. Again his eyes went to his mother. She nodded and he turned around to go and look for Bakoma after saying good bye to the visitors. His love, his Bakoma.

When he walked into his sister's chambers, he saw them talking animatedly about the events of that day. They stopped as soon as he entered and at a sign from her brother, Princess Boatemaa left with the two maids. Bakoma stood facing him trembling. A thousand messages flashed through their eyes to one another in an instant. The most prominent one being that, that love that is meant to be, will surely find a way, no matter how long it took. This is the miracle Bakoma had been praying for. No matter how great the obstacles, no matter the distance, love will always conquer against all odds.

Then as if on cue, they ran into each other's arms. Ecstasy! At last!

"Bakoma, you are mine now. Mine forever!"

He set her down, and with eyes full of love and tenderness, gently laid his lips on hers as they kissed, sealing their love and pledging their allegiance to one another. Forever! But will it be forever?

Glossary

Okyeame:	linguist/spokesman
Oware:	a traditional game played with beads
Ohemaa:	queen
Nana:	title given to a male of the royal family
Opanin:	title given to elderly persons
Fufu:	a dish made of pounded roots and tubers like *cocoyam*, yam, cassava, and or plantain, eaten with soup
Ekyim:	sauce made with spices and meat
Bosoa:	traditional sausage
Apeatuo:	a national levy imposed by the Asante King for specific tasks
Nkwansrafo:	body of scouts
Twafo:	advance guard
Adonten:	main body of the military
Gyaase:	personal bodyguard of a chief
Asantrofie anoma:	a bird known to bring doom to whoever catches it

Bakoma, Princess Adutwumwaa, leaves for her father's village, Kubease, ...with other princes also lying in wait, can this love stand the test of distance, or will their bond be broken? A preview from the next book...

It was a bright sunny day but also chilly because the harmattan air still hung in the air like a blanket. The atmosphere at Kubease was charged with excitement. Men and women in their best cloths had been trooping into the palace courtyard since dawn. This courtyard was large with several rooms opening into different chambers surrounding it. In the center stood the banana plant known to have been planted by Okomfo Anokye when he had visited the place many years ago. This plant was fenced with whitewashed mud bricks. It was around this plant that the numerous friends and well wishers, including gabardine clad white men and the royal family were seated.

Different groups of drummers and singers were playing and singing. The old and the young, especially the women, all in white cloths were dancing gracefully from one end of the courtyard to another. The guards were finding it difficult to control the surge of children into the courtyard.

Soon there was a hush as Princesses Bensuaa and Bakoma were announced. They were preceded into the yard by their maids and several friends followed by some women singing praises to God.

"Osee yee, yee, yee, Twediampon Nyame ei
Yeda wase oo, yeda wase ahenema o
Yen na yenie oo!
Atadwe enne yeate de nne, atadwe, enne yeate de
nne!
Osee yee, yee, yee,
Oh our most reliable God, accept our great thanks
today. We have heard good news today!"

Nana Afua Serwah, the oldest of the women's counselors at the palace led them to shake hands and welcome the guests one after the other. Some of the friends of their late mother hugged Bakoma, exclaiming over her beauty and her resemblance to her late mother. Nana Foriwaa, the queen of Beyam and the closest of them all to their mother stood up with tears in her eyes and declared,

"Ah Adutwumwaa, you're indeed the spitting

image of your mother. Your mother would have been proud of you this day!"

"Thank you Nana." Bakoma who was moved by these declarations, whispered as she moved away from her embrace.

They were led to their seats near their father and the rest of the family after the greetings. Bakoma and her sister were excited and Bensuaa was busy pointing out and mentioning names of other royal houses to her. With all this excitement, Bakoma still longed for the presence of her Prince, Gyakari, wishing he were there. Then she remembered the aftermath of her discovery as a princess back at Nton.

That evening after she and Gyakari had renewed their pledges of love for one another, they had been summoned to the council room where Nana Karikari had informed them that there was nothing standing in their way to be married. But Bakoma had been asked to return with her brother Prince Boakye to Kubease to see her father before any steps towards their betrothal would be taken.

The young ones could hardly keep their eyes off one another as they were being counseled and had desperately wished to be alone since Bakoma was to leave the very next day. So Prince Gyakari had grasped Bakoma's hand and had rushed out of the council room with her as soon as they had been dismissed while others looked on indulgently; many still puzzled over the turn of events that day.

He had plopped Bakoma on his horse, Warrior and after climbing after her, had led the horse out of the palace and galloped to his favorite hideout by the river, followed by Agyei, his personal guard. Agyei was still in a daze not fully believing what had happened that day. One moment his young lord was sorrowfully resigned to the fact of letting Bakoma go and then to find themselves back together.

"Indeed these two are fated to be together." He mused and then came out with an adage that,

"A, egya a eyenam nkye afuo so."

The passion that Gyakari had for Bakoma which he had had to brutally bank because of traditional customs did not hesitate to flare up again. Agyei followed them from a distance giving the two royals privacy.

When they got to the river bank, Gyakari had held out his hands to help Bakoma down from the horse. They had gazed intensely into each other's eyes and had fallen into one another's arms.

Bakoma remembered how Gyakari had squeezed her and had felt him tremble with passion as he had continued to hold her, rocking her from side to side.

Then he had pulled her down beside him on the grass as they continued to gaze at each other. Gyakari had shaken his head in wonder several times not knowing what to say. Finally, he had whispered again and again,

"Bakoma, ah Bakoma. This is like..like a dream." He had paused shaking his head again.

Bakoma just continued to stare at him with a smile, memorizing his facial features for the time when they would be apart.

"Bakoma, did you know that I was all prepared, albeit, reluctantly, to forget you?" She nodded, still dazed and speechless as Gyakari continued,

"And then all of a sudden..out of nowhere..this O this is a miracle! It's a great wonder that just as I was prepared to release you, you've been given back to me," he ended still incredulous.

Then he had pulled her down beside him and had taken her into his arms putting into his kiss, all that he intended to say but couldn't. Bakoma had responded wildly to his kiss, clinging to him and continually saying in her mind that Gyakari belonged to her forever. They had become so engrossed with each other that they had not heard Agyei approaching them. Gyakari broke the kiss but continued to hold her and whispered,

"How on earth am I going to bear your absence,

Bakoma? We have just found each other again."

Bakoma placed her fore finger on his lips interrupting him.

"Hush Gyakari. What is important is that we have each other and you know that I have to go," she replied gently.

He stared down at her for a moment struggling to come to terms with the realities of the impending separation but it was becoming difficult. "So how long will you be gone?" He finally asked.

She shrugged replying, "O I don't really know. I suppose it depends on my father." They sat in silence, each with their own gloomy thoughts as they held onto each other.

Gyakari had then arrived at a decision to make sure that she didn't stay away too long and had decided to speak to her brother Prince Boakye to plead his intentions towards Bakoma to their father. He had sensed that a lot of things could happen after they separated and wanted to take steps to ensure that no one came between himself and his Bakoma.

After arriving at this decision, his heart became lighter though still apprehensive. He would have preferred if they had been formally betrothed but he needed her father's consent first. Then he would have been able to claim her totally, body and soul, binding her completely to himself to ensure that no one walked his turf in his absence but under the circumstances, especially as Bakoma was now a princess, he had to tread carefully.

Bakoma had slowly disengaged herself from his arms and had seen the conflicting emotions warring across his handsome face. She had also struggled to come to terms with the impending separation from him. She knew it was going to be soul wrenching and these thoughts had brought tears to her eyes. Gyakari saw them and suddenly pulled her up with him and taking her head in his hands had whispered anxiously to her,

"Bakoma, promise me..promise that you will return to me." He searched her face in anguish Bakoma could no longer keep back the tears that had been struggling to burst out of her. She sobbed silently feeling his anxiety and anguish and moved quickly to reassure him.

"O Gyakari, of course, I promise..with all..all my heart. There can never be another you..anywhere. I love you very..very much. You know that."

As if he had not heard what she had said, he went on again. "Promise me that you won't allow yourself to be married off to..to another."

Bakoma had never entertained this thought but

suddenly realized that her father, a powerful chief, could betroth her to another prince without her consent. She hugged Gyakari to herself with a sob saying,

"Gyakari, I promise but..but I don't know my father and I don't know what plans he may have for me." She paused and broke the embrace looking intensely up at him and with determination continued, "But I promise I will do everything..everything within my power not to allow that to happen. Do you believe that Gyakari?" She asked in a whisper.

Gyakari had smiled, his heart soaring and had replied "I believe you Bakoma, my Bakoma." Then remembering the token of his necklace he had given to her some months earlier, he had asked her to wear it always as a reminder of his love for her. He had taken her into his arms, molding her to himself and had whispered in her ears, "I love you so much that if..if anything comes between us, I don't know what.." But Bakoma quickly cut in with "Trust me Gyakari that is all I ask." She pulled away searching his face.

"I love you too, very much and as I told you a few months ago before you left for war that this heart of mine beats only for you. There can never be anyone else for me. I'll rather die."

She ended this statement with such vehemence and

eyes flashing that Gyakari had smiled thinking how brave his Bakoma was and had gathered her into his arms, pledging their love for each other and sealing it with a kiss.

All these memories brought a smile to her face but a hard tug at her hand by her sister finally brought Bakoma back to the present.

"Adutwumwaa! Really! What happened to you? You were miles away." Bakoma turned to her smiling without a reply. Her sister narrowed her eyes at her and said "You were thinking about Gyakari again, weren't you?"

She asked with a smile and Bakoma burst out laughing with embarrassment just as a tall muscular man with a powerful aura eased into her vision. Her laughter died in her throat instantly as she felt the hairs at the back of her head rise. She found herself drawn into looking into the most sensual eyes she had ever seen.